moby clique

Also by Cara Lockwood

Wuthering High
The Scarlet Letterman

moby clique

a bard academy novel

cara lockwood

POCKET BOOKS   MTV BOOKS

New York   London   Toronto   Sydney

 BOOKS

A Division of Simon & Schuster, Inc.
1230 Avenue of the Americas
New York, NY 10020

This book is a work of fiction. Names, characters, places, and incidents either are products of the author's imagination or are used fictitiously. Any resemblance to actual events or locales or persons, living or dead, is entirely coincidental.

First MTV Books/Pocket Books trade paperback edition March 2008

POCKET and colophon are registered trademarks
of Simon & Schuster, Inc.

For information about special discounts for bulk purchases, please contact Simon & Schuster Special Sales at 1-800-456-6798 or business@simonandschuster.com

Manufactured in the United States of America

10 9 8 7 6 5 4 3 2 1

ISBN-13: 978-1-4165-5050-1
ISBN-10:   1-4165-5050-X

For all my English teachers

Acknowledgments

A heartfelt thanks to Elizabeth Kinsella, who named this book (second one running!). My great gratitude goes to my husband, Daren, and daughter, Hana, who put up with late-night revisions and much more. I'm grateful to my very savvy editors, Lauren McKenna and Megan McKeever; my agent, Deidre Knight; and everyone at the Knight Agency. Thanks to my parents and my brother, Matt, and the other great supporters of my varsity promotional team: Kate Kinsella, Shannon Whitehead, Stacey Causey, Kate Miller, Jane Ricordati, and Carroll Jordan.

One

Call me bored.

As in—terminally.

I'm a hundred pages into the Longest Book I've Ever Read—*Moby-Dick*—Bard Academy's summer reading requirement. If you ask my opinion, Herman Melville could've shortened this tome by about five hundred pages if he wasn't so long-winded (I mean, twenty pages alone on the *color white*? Yeah, I got it—okay? The whale is WHITE. Sheesh. Get on with it!).

I glance out the grungy window of my Chicago Transit Authority bus seat and see jet skiers and wind-surfers dotting the horizon on Lake Michigan. I have to take the bus to work because my driving privileges are still revoked (see: Dad still holding a grudge about his totaled BMW from a year ago). Looking at the long stretch of water, I find myself wondering what it would be like if that whale came to life. I can almost imagine a wave becoming a giant whale, rising up, and swallowing three jet skiers whole.

A bike darts in front of the bus and the driver slams on the brakes, throwing me forward and nearly making me drop my book. For an instant, I feel adrenaline running through my veins and my muscles tense up, ready for a fight. I half expect Moby Dick or some other menacing fictional character to appear out of nowhere. I have to remind myself that those things don't happen out here in the real world. My heart rate slows down and I take a few deep breaths. I'm not at Bard. Not where ghosts walk the halls and fictional characters come to life. That was just another posttraumatic Bard moment.

But some of you probably never heard of Bard.

Let me recap.

My dad sent me away to delinquent boarding school (Bard Academy) for my sophomore year after wrecking his Beemer. But what he doesn't know is that Bard is not your ordinary, run-of-the-mill boarding school for delinquents. It's staffed with the ghosts of famous writers, and fictional characters sometimes come to life and wander the campus. This is Bard's big secret, but few people know it. Just me and a few of my friends. And by the way, we managed to save the school (oh yeah, and the world) twice from total annihilation. You see, not all the ghosts there are good ghosts. I found that out the hard way.

cara lockwood

I close the book on my lap and take a deep breath. At Bard, some books hold special powers. But out here, away from school, the book is just ordinary, I remind myself. Nothing to worry about.

Still, just in case, I tuck the book snugly into my backpack. You never know.

I glance out the window and recognize the strip shopping mall where I work. I'm about to miss my stop. I grab my bag and push open the back door, then step out into a humid August day. There, glaring at me in hot pink, is the sign I've come to hate. It reads "In the Pink" and it hangs above the store that belongs to my Dad's third wife, Carmen. I've been forced to work here all summer without pay to help "offset my Bard tuition," which is how Dad puts it. I never thought I'd see something scarier than some of the ghosts I'd come face-to-face with at Bard Academy, but Carmen's shop is one big horror show. There are pink plush toys, pink garters, pink toothbrushes—and (serious *ew* here) pink edible underwear. It's nice to know that instead of saving for my college education, Dad has opted to fritter my tuition away on inflatable flamingos and posters of pigs in ballet tutus. Clearly, In the Pink (or, as I like to call it, In the Puke) is of so much more social significance than, say, me becoming a doctor and one day curing cancer. Not that I would, but In the Pink definitely isn't going to.

"You're late," Carmen says to me the minute I walk through the door. She's snapping pink bubble gum at me as she tosses a pink, furry boa over my head. This is what she forces employees (i.e., me) to wear. I glance up at the clock.

"Technically, I'm an hour early," I tell her, nodding at the giant neon pink clock in the shape of lips on the wall.

"You know that clock doesn't work," Carmen snaps.

"Like half of the stuff in here," I mumble, but she doesn't hear me.

"Honestly, Miranda. If you were mine, I would seriously think about disowning you," she says. This is Carmen's idea of being warm. My "stepmom," who hasn't been able to keep a goldfish alive and has the mothering instincts of a brick, is twenty-six. That's not even a decade older than I am. This is why I sometimes call Dad a pedophile just to see him get mad. It works every time.

I ignore her and take up my place behind the cash register. I plunk down my bag and open up *Moby-Dick*. There aren't exactly dozens of people clamoring to buy broken lip clocks.

"Reading? Again?" Carmen scoffs. "I don't know what's gotten into you since you've been back from Bard Academy, but you're reading *way* too much. You

cara lockwood

know reading causes you to have to wear glasses. And that would just spoil your whole face."

I want to tell her that never having read a book in her life has probably spoiled her whole brain, but I managed to bite my tongue. Comments like that just make their way straight back to Dad, and then he threatens to send me off to juvenile detention. As it is, I'm just three days away from heading back to Bard Academy for my junior year. Normally, I'd be dreading it. But, recently, I've found myself actually wanting to get back to Bard.

In some ways, the real world just seems so, well, *boring.* Besides, at Bard, I'm someone special. Turns out I'm part fiction, distantly related to Catherine of *Wuthering Heights* fame. At Bard, I'm more than just my dad's child support payment or Carmen's surly employee. I really am someone. Someone who saved the school. Twice. Here, I'm just one more underappreciated adolescent taking the bus and working a grunt job.

"Anyway, I've told you *a million times* that you can't read while we have customers," Carmen scolds as she wraps a long piece of her newly highlighted hair around one finger.

I glance up and around the store. There are no customers. Not unless you count the eighty-year-old woman who's been nosing around the fifty-percent-off

bin. As I look up, she picks up a pack of edible underwear, sniffs it, and then drops it back in the bin.

Gross.

"No reading while we have customers," Carmen
says. "We have an image to uphold."

I can think of a million smart things to say here. Like
the fact that I'm sorry to be reading when we've got
such a *stampede* of customers lining around the block
to buy pink Post-it notes that say "Queen of Pink" on
them. Or the fact that I can't see how *Moby-Dick* would
do anything but improve the image of a store in a strip
shopping mall stuffed between a dry cleaner's and a
Dunkin Donuts.

Instead, I settle for, "Oh yes, we're the model of so-
phistication," while I hold up a pink roll of condoms in
a package shaped like a lollypop.

"Shut up," she snaps, because Carmen never can
think of anything smart to say back to me. Dad certainly didn't marry her for her sparkling personality,
that's for sure. She grabs the neon condoms out of my
hand and puts them on a nearby shelf.

Three more days. Only *three* more days. And then I
am out of here and back to Bard, and to . . . my complicated love life. In one corner, there's my ex, Ryan
Kent, state championship basketball player. Gorgeous.
Smart. Sweet. And totally uninterested in dating me
anymore. In the other corner, there's Heathcliff. Brood-

ing. Mysterious. Serious bad-boy mojo. And completely off-limits because he's a) a fictional character, and b) did I mention he's fiction? He is the original bad boy from *Wuthering Heights* and the Bard faculty told me explicitly that I couldn't date him because he doesn't belong in this world.

Most girls my age have to worry about whether or not the boy of their dreams knows they exist. I have to worry whether or not my boy actually *does* exist. It's a strange, strange world.

I put my hand to the locket I wear around my neck, the one that contains a bit of a page from *Wuthering Heights*. It's the one thing that's keeping Heathcliff in this world. If it were destroyed, he'd be sent straight back to his fictional universe. That he gave it to me speaks volumes about how much he trusts me—especially since Heathcliff normally doesn't trust anyone.

The shop bell dings and my dad walks through. Reflexively, I frown. Dad and I do not get along. That's because Dad has the emotional maturity of a fourth-grader. And I like to point this out. Often.

"There's my baby!" he says in his exaggerated enthusiasm reserved only for Carmen. He gives her a leer, which makes him look like a lecherous old man. His bald head gleams in the pink fluorescent lights of the store.

"Honey bear!" she cries, and she runs over to give

him a sloppy kiss. Tongue is involved, and I feel like I'm going to vomit. I long for the days when Dad and Carmen fought. That was before Dad dropped a hundred Gs on In the Puke. That's paid for probably a lot more than French kisses. The thought makes me want to wretch. There's only one thing worse than imagining your own parents having sex, and that's imagining them having sex with someone else.

He doesn't acknowledge my presence at all for a full five minutes while he and Carmen exchange sickeningly sweet baby talk. Just when I feel like I'm very close to putting my own eye out with one of Carmen's pink fuzzy disco ball pens, Dad looks up and sees me.

"How's my little *worker* today?" Even Dad can't manage to keep the sarcasm from his voice. "She hasn't caused you any trouble today, has she, Carmen?"

I haven't caused trouble the whole freakin' summer. Not that Dad would notice. Even now, he's already distracted by the edible underwear display. He doesn't even have the attention span to listen to Carmen's answer. Not that I want his attention. If he's not ignoring me, that means he's threatening to send me off to juvie.

"She's been fine, although you know she's reading too much," Carmen says. "It's a distraction for the customers."

"Oh yeah, and that isn't?" I mumble, glancing over

cara lockwood

at the bachelorette section with the giant blow-up pink penis. You know, because little old ladies who are shopping for pink stationery and pink ballpoint pens are also in the market for a giant pink pecker. Only Carmen would think those two go together. And maybe for her they do. She was the one, after all, who would have sex with my dad on the office copier back when he was married to his second wife. Maybe she just associates sex with office products.

"Um-hmmmm," Dad says, clearly not listening, as he picks up a packet of edible strawberry thongs. Serious ew factor. "By the way, where's my other daughter?"

"You mean Lindsay?" I say. I wonder if he's temporarily forgotten my sister's name. I wouldn't put it past him. He's always forgetting our birthdays. Our names wouldn't be much of a stretch.

"I thought she was with you," Carmen says.

Dad shrugs. "She's not with me. . . ."

I sigh. "I don't suppose *either* of you remembered to pick her up from tennis camp? It ended this morning."

Lindsay had insisted on going to some tennis camp this summer. Lindsay had never hit a tennis ball in her life, but that didn't stop her from signing up. Apparently, all the cool kids from her school went, because the most popular girl in her class also happened to be on the varsity team. Lindsay was always chasing after the popular kids. It was so sad and pathetic, really. She never really fit in, but that didn't stop her from sucking up to them all the same. And that's why they kept her around, as far as I could see. She was their personal slave—doing their homework, running their errands, at their beck and call night or day.

"Camp?" Dad echoes, memory starting to dawn. "Was I supposed to pick her up? Or was your mother?"

"Mom said it was your turn," I say. I glance at my watch. If nobody remembered to pick her up, she'd been staring at empty tennis courts at Northwestern for close to five hours. Poor Lindsay. "Didn't she call you?" I ask Dad.

"I haven't had my phone on," he says, shrugging.

Great. Am I the only adult here? If Dad hadn't confiscated my phone as punishment for talking back to Carmen in June, Lindsay could've called me.

"I *told* you you were supposed to go," Carmen tells Dad, who frowns.

"Why couldn't *you* pick her up, then, if you remembered?" he snaps at her, his good mood suddenly gone. "How am I supposed to remember everything?"

"I've got a *business* to run, in case you haven't noticed," Carmen spits.

And then, while Dad and Carmen are arguing about who's responsible for this latest child-rearing debacle

(I swear, neither one of them is responsible enough to raise gerbils), I hear a tap on the glass at the front window.

I look up to see Lindsay standing there, looking peeved, her hands on her hips and her hair a bit of a mess. I don't know how she got here, but chances are none of those popular kids gave her a ride. They usually just ask for favors, they don't grant them. Maybe she took the el? In any case, I guess she got tired of waiting.

She sticks her tongue out at me, like she's always done since she was five. Lindsay doesn't like the fact that I don't approve of her desperate attempts to be popular. That is so not my scene. I'm the artsy, thrift-store girl, not the buy-anything-with-a-designer-label kind of girl. Still, I keep trying to tell Lindsay she's better off not being a popular drone, but she won't listen to me. Even now she looks like she's trying too hard in her head-to-toe Lacoste tennis ensemble. I don't know how she ever convinced Mom to buy it. But Lindsay always gets whatever she wants, including a one-hundred-and-twenty-five-dollar tennis skirt that she'll only wear once. Lindsay typically always tries to play the "good kid" card by pointing out how bad I am, and she usually gets the parentals to buy her whatever she wants.

She jangles keys in the window. They're Dad's spare

car keys that he keeps in a magnetized tin box underneath his bumper. I'd recognize the key chain anywhere. It's one of Carmen's. It's a pink furry slipper.

"Um, guys . . . ?" I say, trying to interrupt Carmen and Dad, who are still going at it. Those two argue as crassly as they make out. It's really kind of gross.

As I watch, Lindsay flips Dad off (although Dad can't see) and then climbs into the driver's seat of his brand-new shiny Land Rover. I don't know what she thinks she's doing. She's fourteen. The most driving experience she's ever had is playing Mario Kart.

"Dad," I say, starting to worry now. She looks like she's turning over the engine. I hear his Land Rover rev. "Lindsay's over there. She's in your car."

"She's *what*!" Dad shouts, just as Lindsay sticks out her tongue at the three of us, and then turns around as if she has the car in reverse. But she doesn't. She's got the car in drive, and faster than you can say "*The Fast and the Furious,*" she's run straight into the window of In the Puke, shattering glass everywhere and nearly running over the little old lady by the sales bin. The front bumper of the Land Rover comes to a screeching halt about a foot from the counter where we're standing. Lindsay has a look of surprise on her face, too. I'm guessing she didn't quite mean to actually run through the store. She meant to steal Dad's car, only she didn't know which gear was which.

cara lockwood

I'm the first to recover from my shock, and I glance over at Carmen, who looks like Macaulay Culkin from the original *Home Alone* movies. She's got both her hands on her face and her mouth in a big, round O. Dad is turning various shades of red and purple. He can't even form words he's so mad.

This can't be good.

"Uh, Dad, this is like *totally* Miranda's fault," Lindsay sputters, pointing to me. "She's a bad influence!"

TWO

"So what is Bard *like*?" Lindsay asks me for the hundredth time since we started the trip to Bard Academy.

This was Dad's idea of punishing her—sending her along with me to Bard Academy. Only it's far more a punishment for me, because Lindsay simply will not be quiet. She's literally not shut up since we got to the airport, and since then we've been on a bus and we're now on a boat taking us to Shipwreck Island, home to Bard Academy. Of course, Dad knew it would suck for me. That's why he did it. Lindsay did blame me for her little car stunt, and Dad, as usual, believed her. This is because Lindsay is the "nice" daughter and I'm the one with the "bad attitude."

"I *asthed* you a *quethyon*," Lindsay lisps. The lisp is from her retainer, which she wears twenty-four/seven. She's the only person I know who actually *follows* her orthodontist's instructions. She's convinced that having perfect teeth is the ticket to being popular. She didn't even really need the retainer, but insisted on one because one of the popular kids once hinted she had a bit of an overbite. Naturally, trying to explain that this kid was probably just trying to get under Lindsay's skin didn't fly.

"Hello—*earff* to Miranda!" she trills.

A bit of her spittle falls on my arm.

"You're spitting on me!" I cry, wiping it away.

"Thorry," she says. *"Tho?* What'*th* the deal?"

"It's a delinquent boarding school, so it's got a lot of delinquents," I say for the hundredth time. How else do you explain Bard? First off, I can't exactly tell her what the school is really like. I can't spill the big secret, which is that it's actually a kind of literary purgatory.

"But what *kind* of delinquents?"

Lindsay is taking far too great an interest in the wayward brethren of the school. I'm going to have to tell Mom about this. Of course, I can't believe Mom let her favorite child go in the first place, but she put up a minimal fuss. She's been too distracted lately by her blazing love affair with Mr. Perkins, Lindsay's math teacher.

"You'll see when we get there. It's Gothic and boring and strict, okay?"

"Like Gothic how? Like *Picture of Dorian Gray* Gothic?"

I glance at her. "You read *Picture of Dorian Gray*?"

"Duh—last year. I got MacKenzie an A on her paper."

MacKenzie is the queen bee at Lindsay's school and Lindsay literally worships her.

"You shouldn't write papers for her," I scold. "You ought to let her do that herself."

"She's my *friend*," Lindsay says, crossing her arms and jutting out her chin.

"She's not your friend," I snap. "She's just using you."

"What*ever*," Lindsay says, sticking her lower lip out in a pout. She's mad at me, but on the bright side, maybe she'll be quiet.

"Do you think we'll be roommates?" she asks after a second. There goes quiet.

"No," I say. "You're a freshman. I'm a junior."

"So are there gangs at the school? And drugs? And fights?" Lindsay seems to really dig the idea of going to school with a thug element. I'm not sure where this is coming from. For most of her life she's been safely tucked into her honors classes.

"Why are you so obsessed with delinquents?"

"Well, I don't know any, except for you. I just think it would be cool to know some."

I think about Parker Rodham, one of the richest girls at the school, who is also accused of poisoning her mother. There is nothing cool about her, unless you think ruthless evil is cool.

"Are you serious?" I ask her.

"Duh," she says, rolling her eyes. "My old school was boring. I'm glad I'm going with you."

I can't believe this. My wannabe prom queen sister is actually stoked about being sent away to delinquent boarding school. Unbelievable. My dad thought this would be such a punishment for her, but she actually *likes* the idea of being a tough girl.

I look at her and I can't believe we're sisters. For one thing, we only share a passing resemblance. We have the same pale complexion, and nearly the same height, but beyond that, I'm skinnier and Lindsay has all the curves. The girl developed at thirteen, whereas I'm basically still waiting. And while I'm wearing clothes of the punk chick-meets-Sienna Miller variety, she looks like a car wreck between two warring prep gangs. Basically, Martha's Vineyard meets Orange County, which is trademark MacKenzie style.

"Lindsay, there's a seriously bad element at the school, you know," I warn her. "You have to be careful."

"I will," Lindsay promises. "But you're there to protect me, so I'm not too scared. Besides, don't you have that boyfriend of yours? What's his name? Heathcliff?"

"How do you know about Heathcliff?" I ask her sharply.

She shrugs. "I've only been reading your mail. And your password-protected blog."

"Why, you little . . ." I can't believe she hacked into my computer! I'd been keeping an offline blog of sorts, just to try to sort out my feelings. Besides, Ms. W said I should keep a diary or journal, to help me deal with life in general.

"But what happened to that Ryan guy? I thought you were gaga over him."

"None of your business."

Even I don't know quite how I feel about my ex these days. Or about Heathcliff, for that matter.

"I thought you weren't even *allowed* to date," Lindsay says, referring to the fact that my parents forbade me to date at the end of freshman year when I snuck out of the house to meet a boy who tried to get me drunk.

The ferry horn blows, signaling the fact that we're closing in on Shipwreck Island and Bard Academy. Lindsay grabs her massive backpack and pulls out a folder with printouts she's made of her research of Shipwreck Island. She's always well organized. It's how she keeps all the papers she's doing for other people straight.

"You know it was supposed to be a place where pirates hung out," Lindsay says, showing me the fruits of her Google search. "It's rumored there's even an old pirate ship there. In a place called Whale Cove."

"Is not," I say, whipping the printout from her hand.

Lindsay shrugs. "*Tho* don't believe me. What do I care? Anyway, how deep do you think that water *ith*?" she asks, looking over the side of the boat where the dark, cold water sloshes against the side of the hull. For some reason, it's always foggy and overcast every time I make this trip, so the water between Maine and Shipwreck Island always looks inky black.

"I don't know," I say. "I think it's creepy, though."

"I think it's cool," Lindsay says, leaning nearly as far over the railing as she can so she can get a look down below. I grab her by the belt loops and pull her back down.

"Close your mouth or your retainer is going to fall out," I warn. "And you'll fall in after it."

"What*ever,*" Lindsay lisps, spitting a little as she talks. She glances up and points to a single figure standing on the shore. "Who'*th* that?"

I know even before I get close enough to see his face that those big, broad shoulders belong to Heathcliff. He's not allowed to leave the island, so he's been stuck there all summer. My heart speeds up a little bit. I wonder how long he's been waiting there for me. He runs a hand through his thick, jet-black hair and then holds his hand there as if to shade it from the overcast sky. He's as dark and magnetic as ever. I throw up my arm to wave at him and he does the same. I didn't realize until this moment just how much I missed him.

"Is that him? Is that Heathcliff?" Lindsay chirps beside me, jumping up and down and making a spectacle of herself. "You didn't tell me he was so hot!"

Other people are starting to stare at Lindsay's theatrics, probably because they've never seen anyone as hyper as my sister before. As we move in closer, Heathcliff gives my sister a quizzical glance, but nothing more than a glance. His eyes are fixed directly on me. I don't think they leave me at all. I can feel them on me as I grab my bags and head down the gangplank to shore.

A slow smile spreads across my face as I get nearer to Heathcliff, who is standing very still on the beach, his hands stuffed in his pockets. I can't read his expression exactly, but I think he's glad to see me. When I'm face-to-face with him, though, I feel a sudden awkwardness.

"Hi," I manage shyly. Heathcliff has that effect on me. I lose my ability to speak clearly. Behind me, I hear Lindsay struggling with one of her four bags. I'm determined to let her struggle. I told her not to bring too much luggage, but the girl insisted on bringing half the Nordstrom juniors' department.

"Hey," he says back, and then grabs my bag.

"So how long have you been waiting for me?" I ask, teasing.

"All summer," he says, completely serious. He reaches up and gently tucks a stray piece of hair behind my ear. His touch makes me shiver. And there's something about him that makes all the words in my head simply dry up and disappear. But Heathcliff doesn't seem to mind the lack of conversation. He is, after all, the strong and silent type.

Lindsay interrupts the Hallmark moment, though, as she finally catches up to me, huffing and puffing with her bags, and being her usual annoying self.

"*Thankth* for the *help*," she says sarcastically, dropping her bags around her and accidentally landing one on Heathcliff's foot. Heathcliff doesn't even flinch, he just glances at the bag and then at Lindsay, a curious look on his face.

"I'm sorry about that," I say, quickly tugging Lindsay's heavy bag off his foot. "This is my—"

Before I can finish, Lindsay has prattled on, spitting as she talks. "*Tho*, you're Heathcliff? I've heard *all* about you," she says. "You're like *totally* a tough guy, right? I mean, what did you do to get *th*ent here? Did you kill *th*omeone? You can tell me if you did, because I will *totally* not tell anyone. I mean, Miranda *thays* I can't keep a *th*ecret, that's *th*uch a lie. I *totally* can.

I mean, you had to do *th*omething really bad, right? Miranda said you can fight and stuff, and she is like, *totally,* into you, which i*th* crazy because it'*th* not like Dad would let her ever date a delinquent. I mean, no offense or anything, but you do look at least twenty-four, and how old did you *th*ay you were again?"

I worry how Heathcliff might react. He's not known for his patience. But he doesn't look angry, just puzzled. My sister has that effect on a lot of people.

"And I've read all about you because Miranda won't *th*op . . ." She's literally spraying Heathcliff with spit.

I step on Lindsay's foot, hard. "OW!" she cries. "What'd you do that for?"

"You're *spitting,*" I say.

"What! It's not my fault," she says. And then she does the unthinkable. She takes *out* her retainer and actually holds it up for Heathcliff to see. He looks at it like she just threw up an alien. She wipes it on her jeans and then she actually puts it *back* in her mouth.

"This," I say and sigh, "is my little sister, Lindsay."

Heathcliff nods slowly.

"I don't know why you did that," Lindsay is saying, rubbing her foot. "I mean, it'*th* not like violence ever *th*olves anything. Of cour*th,* Heathcliff might disagree, and, I mean, like no offen*th* or anything, but brute force i*th* just not where it'*th* at. Besides, it'*th* not even like I told him anything really embarra*th*ing, like how you scribbled hi*th* name a million times in your journal and you—"

"Lindsay!" I shout, exasperated.

"What? I'm just *thaying* you *th*ouldn't keep your feeling*th* in all the time. Maybe if you let them out once in a while you wouldn't be *th*uch a basket case. Ooh! I*th* that the bu*th*? Are we going on that bu*th* to the *th*cool? It'*th* kind of *th*mall for all of us. I wonder if they have room for my bag*th*."

Lindsay runs up ahead to the bus that's parked near the dock, leaving us alone with her four giant bags.

"Does she always talk this much?" Heathcliff asks me, looking a little bewildered.

"I'm afraid so," I say, and sigh.

Three

In the campus chapel during orientation, Lindsay is the only one actually taking notes as Headmaster B runs through the usual list of Bard no-no's (no cell phones, computers, games, or anything else that runs on batteries and/or would possibly distract or entertain you). Heathcliff keeps sneaking glances at my sister, as if he can't believe the two of us are related. I can't either, actually. For her part, she shows absolutely no fear when it comes to Heathcliff (actually telling him to sit up straight, asking him why he never speaks more than one-word answers to questions, and the endless pestering about what he did to be sent to Bard in the first place). Honestly, I don't think Heathcliff has ever run into somebody who feared him less. Most people in the school give Heathcliff a wide berth. He is the one, after all, who took out three school Guardians by himself, not to mention the things I've seen him do (wrestle with Dracula, for starters). But Lindsay shows no fear. At this rate, she's going to last two days at Bard.

"There you are!" Blade cries, finding the three of us in the crowd after orientation, while the church empties out to the lines of boys and girls where our bags will be searched. Blade is my former roomie and also a self-professed Wiccan witch. On a Goth scale of one to ten, she's an eleven. Since I've last seen her, she's dyed her hair black with red streaks, and over the summer has gotten a new set of eyebrow piercings. She's also wearing a chain that connects her left eyebrow to her nose ring. You'd think she had done something really bad to be sent here. Come to find out, it's mainly because she likes putting up pictures of Satan on her walls to get under the skin of her father, who happens to be a pastor.

"Doesn't that hurt when you raise your eyebrow?" I ask her, pointing to her latest face piercing.

"Nah, not anymore," Blade says. "Hey, who's this?"

My sister, Lindsay, for once, has shut up, and she's just staring at Blade, her mouth open. It may be the eyebrow ring, or the black lipstick, or the fact that Blade's sporting a red pentagram on her cheek in lipstick.

"Wow—you are *tho* cool" is all Lindsay can say, mouth open in awe.

"Hardly," says Hana, who joins us. Hana was the first person I met at Bard and the closest thing to a best friend I have here. I throw my arms around her and give her a squeeze. "Whoa, let me breathe, girl," she says, backing up a bit. She's also the one I've been IMing all summer, and I feel like we've never been apart. Her summer was filled with family drama—as in, a lack thereof. Her parents spent the summer in Switzerland, leaving her alone in their New York penthouse suite. Hana was sent to Bard mainly because she got kicked out of other boarding schools and her parents can't be bothered to deal. I don't have time to ask Hana about her little brother (the one she'd been babysitting for the better part of the summer), before Samir joins us. He's our group's resident goofball.

"My man H!" Samir cries, putting up a fist for Heathcliff to meet. Only Heathcliff just leaves Samir hanging, giving him a dirty look. Like I said before, Heathcliff is the original brooding bad boy. "Er, right, well, maybe they didn't have that in 1847."

"What?" asks Lindsay, confused.

"He's joking," I say quickly. The last thing I want to do is get into the big secret with Lindsay.

"Guys, this is my kid sister, Lindsay. Lindsay—that's Hana and Samir and Blade."

"Like, ohmigod, *real* delinquents," Lindsay says,

rubbing her hands together in glee. "*Th*o, like, tell me, what did you guy*th* do to get *th*ent here?"

"Are you sure you two are related?" Hana asks me as the two of us unpack our suitcases in the senior girls' dorm. She's my roommate this year, because Blade went off to room with one of her Goth friends, who's a witch-in-training. Blade said she felt bad about abandoning me, but at the same time felt the need to stay true to her Wiccan roots. Honestly, I don't mind. Blade's idea of room décor is pictures of skulls and Satan. Plus, most of her "spells" smell like old gym socks.

"I think she was switched with my real sister at birth," I say, shaking my head.

"You think she's going to be okay?" Hana asks me.

The last time we saw her was when we dropped her off at her dorm, which is next door to ours.

"I don't know," I say. "I just hope she doesn't get in trouble, which she's prone to do, especially if she goes around asking everybody why they're delinquents."

"Yeah, that's not the sort of thing to win you friends among the criminal set," Hana says. "And there are plenty of those types at Bard."

She's right. The school mostly falls into six basic cliques: druggies, freaks, Goths, kleptos, jocks/date rapists, and white-collar criminals (the extremely rich kids). The lst group doesn't need Bard Academy scholarships (offered up to thirty percent of the student body), and everybody knows they are the absolute worst offenders. Ironically, they also seem like the most clean cut.

Hana, Samir, and I stay out of the cliques for the most part. Blade has her Goth friends, but we don't usually hang with them. I wonder how Lindsay is going to fit in.

"Miranda Tate, are you sure you've got the right room?" purrs the unmistakably evil voice of Parker Rodham, interrupting my thoughts. Parker is standing in our doorway looking her usual viper self, her sleek blond hair pulled up tight in a ponytail, her makeup flawless, and she's clad from head to toe in Burberry.

Parker, a.k.a. queen of the white-collar kids, is rumored to have poisoned her mother and nearly killed her, as well as murdered two of her ex-boyfriends in convenient "accidents." She also happens to hate my guts for dating Ryan Kent last semester, because she's been pining over him since he transferred to Bard.

"Parker, what are you doing here?" I ask.

"I was about to ask you the same question," she says.

Immediately, I realize my mistake. I've moved into her turf, not the other way around. Last year, she was in the upperclassman dorm, and I was in the underclassman dorm, and now I've moved up a level.

"It looks like we're *neighbors*," Parker's roommate

says, nodding to their room across the hall. She's one of Parker's clones, a girl who essentially has no identity other than to look and sound exactly like Parker.

"You live there?" Hana asks, her face falling. She has no love for Parker, either. And she knows exactly what kind of bad news it is that Parker is living right across the hall.

"Miranda!" I hear my sister shout in her telltale lisp. "Miranda! Where *are* you? Miranda!"

Oh God. She's found me somehow. And in front of Parker, no less. And she's not even supposed to be *in* this dorm. She'll get us both in trouble.

"Looks like you've got a fan," Parker says, and gives me a slow, calculating smile.

Lindsay runs up to my door and nearly collides straight into Parker. "Um, *tho*rry," she lisps. "I need to talk to my *thith*ter."

Parker looks at Lindsay like she's a cockroach, taking in Lindsay's pressed pastel Polo shirt and khakis. "*This* is your sister?" Parker asks me, an amused look on her face. God, this is so embarrassing. Not that I care what Parker thinks, but why does Lindsay have to be so, well, embarrassing? "Nice shirt," Parker says, but she clearly means the opposite.

"Oh, thank*th*! I've got a whole clo*th*et full," Lindsay says, beaming. "I'm Lind*th*ay," my sister says quickly, sticking out her hand for a shake. Parker gives it a disdainful look, but then decides to shake it.

"I'm Parker," she says. "Now, if you need *anything,* you let me know, okay, Lindsay?"

"Um, okay, thank*th,*" Lindsay says, nodding.

"I mean it—I'm only here to help," Parker says, venom dripping from her smile. "Any sister of Miranda's . . . well, you know the rest. We'll see you around."

Parker nods at us both and then retreats to her room across the hall, where I can hear her and her clone cackling. They think Lindsay is hilarious. Lindsay, meanwhile, is oblivious.

"She's nice," Lindsay says. "And she has cool clothes."

"No, she's evil and she has evil clothes," I correct. "And you should stay away from her. Now, what's the problem?"

"You have any tampon*th*? I'm all out," Lindsay says at a volume not fit for discussions about feminine products. She's so loud, in fact, that I hear Parker and her clone across the hall dissolve into another fit of snorts and giggles.

Ms. P (as in Sylvia Plath), our dorm mother, the faculty member in charge of the girls' upperclassman dorm, makes an appearance in the hall, just as Lindsay is rummaging through my suitcase.

"Miranda Tate," Ms. P calls, and then stalks with a purpose straight toward me. Her dark blond hair falls in ringlets at her shoulders and she's wearing a plain brown skirt and white blouse. She's also got her tell-tale red lipstick on and very little eye makeup. I've only seen Ms. P in passing on campus, and never had any of her classes, but she always struck me as one of the ghosts who didn't like being stuck at Bard. Not that most of them enjoy purgatory, but some of them are resigned. Ms. P just seems sad. More than sad. Bitter.

Not to mention, my advisor, Ms. W (Virginia Woolf), already warned me that not all the faculty like me. I have two strikes against me because a) I know the secret of Bard, as well as the location of the book vault, which holds the teachers/ghosts' souls, and b) I'm a descendant of a fictional character from *Wuthering Heights*—Catherine Earnshaw's now-lost twin daughter, Elizabeth. Since she left the book to marry my great-great-great-great grandfather, she's no longer in any version you can read now. The faculty doesn't trust fictionistas—people descended from fictional characters. Mainly because we have special powers, since we span both worlds. Last year, Emily Brontë tried to use me to open up the seam between this world and the fictional one. I didn't want to help her, but among some faculty I'm to blame regardless.

"Miranda—back for more punishment?" Ms. P says, putting her hands on her hips and stopping in front of my door.

cara lockwood

"Wow—I love that sweater," Lindsay says, turning on her full brownnosing mode, the way she always does when in the presence of authority. "It really brings out the color of your eyes. And, oooh, is that cashmere?"

Ms. P gives her a look that I would classify as almost warm. Granted, Ms. P isn't smiling—she never smiles—but she's not frowning, either. "It is, actually," she says, then turns to me. "You realize that having an underclassman in this dorm violates Bard procedures."

"I know, Ms. P, but it's my sister and she had a, well, a personal emergency," I say, thinking that her whole life is just one big personal emergency. I mean, *look* at her. She has wrapped tampons sticking out of her jeans and she's still trying to win brownie points. The girl has no shame.

"I'm sorry, Miranda," Ms. P says, crossing her arms. "I can't allow any exceptions to the rules."

"But, Ms. P," Hana starts, trying to defend me.

"That's enough, you two. Miranda and Hana, since this is your room and you have an underclassman in it, you'll be on the first shift to clean the hallways and the bathrooms. You'll be expected to do this every morning *before* breakfast. I expect them to be spotless. Cleaning supplies are in my room, and you'll be reporting there tomorrow morning at five-thirty."

"But—"

"If I hear any more excuses from you, I'll make it two weeks instead of one," Ms. P says curtly. "And as for *you*," she adds, turning to Lindsay. "You get a warning—*this* time. But I expect you to stay out of this dorm, understood?"

"Why does she get a warning and we don't?" I can't believe this. I knew my parents spoiled Lindsay, but why is Ms. P giving her a break?

"You're an expert on Bard, aren't you, Miranda? You should know by now that things here are hardly fair. For any of us." Ms. P gives me a look that tells me she's talking about herself. She's one disgruntled ghost.

I sigh.

It's going to be one long semester.

Four

"Remind me again why Lindsay's not here with us cleaning?" Hana asks me as the two of us stand over a very old-looking toilet seat. This is the most disgusting thing I've ever had to do, hands down, even including stocking the edible undies and inflatable penises at In the Puke.

"Because she's the original kiss-up," I say. "She was practically slobbering over Ms. P trying to win her over. That's why she's my parents' favorite, by the way. Because she's always telling them how great they are, too, even though it's all BS."

"Well, your parents must have caught on. She ended up here, didn't she?"

"But she *wanted* to come here," I say. "She engineered the whole thing. She thought it was some kind of cool private school with a bunch of tough kids. She's in a delinquent phase."

"Still, it's got to be better to have your sister here than not. I wish I could see my brother more often," Hana says.

"But you don't understand. Lindsay blames me for everything and somehow everyone always believes her. I'm always the one getting punished, while Lindsay gets *whatever* she wants. I ask for a hamster and get denied, but Lindsay gets a hamster farm, two gerbils, and a dog. I ask for an iPod Mini and get turned down, but Lindsay not only gets an iPhone, she gets speakers *and* her own laptop, too. I mean, it's just not fair. She gets everything she wants. She even has boobs."

"You have boobs," Hana points out.

"Barely," I say. "She's got B cups, and she's only fourteen. Do you have any idea how embarrassing it is when people assume *she's* the older sister because she's stacked?"

"No, but—"

"And don't even get me started on her popular kids obsession."

I realize I'm scrubbing the toilet a little too hard, and I stop. I'm still so mad that Lindsay followed me to Bard. That's it, really. I feel like she's going to great lengths to ruin my life. Ever since she learned to walk she's been following me around and embarrassing me. Like the time she followed me to Brad Jacobs's house, my fourth-grade crush, and fell into his swimming pool a split second before I swear he was going to kiss me.

And now I'm going to be late for the crummy Bard breakfast because I'm scrubbing toilets.

"At least we can see outside," Hana says, nodding to a big window in the girls' bathroom. We didn't have one of those in our old bathroom. It was wall-to-wall creepy black-and-white tile. This one at least has some light coming in.

I walk over to the window where Hana is standing and see people from across campus filing into the cafeteria, which has just opened.

"Hey, isn't that Lindsay?" Hana points to a girl who does look a lot like my sister. She is, in fact, and she's changed into her Bard Academy uniform. She has her hair up in pigtails, which makes her look twelve, but it's the hairstyle that MacKenzie said looked best on her. Lindsay is such a sucker sometimes. MacKenzie just wanted to make sure Lindsay didn't look prettier than she did, and encouraging Lindsay to look like a kindergartener did the trick. She's also wearing her striped Hollister leg warmers, even though it's not even cold out. And, I notice, she's wearing my Steve Maddens. "And isn't she talking to . . ."

"Parker Rodham," I say. It's true. The two seem to be actually talking. I stiffen, but it doesn't seem like Parker is in her fighting stance. In fact, she and her clone posse are smiling at Lindsay.

"They don't look like they're about to fight," Hana says, voicing my thoughts aloud. "It seems like they're pretty friendly."

"But why? Why is Parker being nice to Lindsay?"

"Maybe they both share a passion for Hollister?"

"I doubt it," I say. "Something is up, and I don't like it."

I don't get a chance to talk to my sister about Parker because by the time we're finished scrubbing toilets I've missed breakfast, and by morning assembly, I can't seem to find her. We're all crowded into the campus chapel again, sitting in pews surrounded by giant stained glass windows. I glance up at them and see the familiar scenes from Shakespeare—*Macbeth, Hamlet,* and *Romeo and Juliet.* Some people might think they're pretty, but to me they just look like one more bad memory.

"Creepy, aren't they?" Hana asks me, nudging me with one arm. She and I both remember last semester when some of those stained glass figures came to life. They weren't so pretty when they were trying to kill us.

"Definitely," I say.

I glance away from MacBeth, who's giving me the creeps, and manage to lock eyes with Ryan Kent. His steady blue eyes meet mine and don't look away.

I thought I was on the road to recovery when it came to him, but now, as I look at his perfectly tanned face, I feel my stomach lurch. I forgot how good he looked.

It's always a shock to see Ryan, because he's gorgeous, in a straight-off-the-set-of-*Laguna Beach* sort of way. He's got beach-blond hair and a gleaming white surfer's smile.

I remember what it felt like to wear his letterman's jacket last year. How he used to look at me before he'd dunk a basketball when I sat in the stands, cheering him on. Back then, I thought we were made for each other. Of course, that was before all the rumors about us circulated—the ones that said I was into things like doing the entire basketball team just to get into Ryan's good graces. Said rumors were started by Parker, of course. She'd do or say anything to try to break us up, since she'd wanted Ryan for herself.

Ryan gives me a hesitant smile, and my stomach flips. I remember the last thing he said to me before summer break: "Let's just be friends for now, and see how things go." So far, I'm thinking, the going is lousy.

I return his smile, but the smile is frozen on my face as I realize Parker Rodham is sitting right next to him. But of course she is. I'm sure they'll be dating before the end of the first week of classes. I feel something dark and oily at the pit of my stomach. Is it jealousy?

And then, on the other side of Ryan, I see . . . Lindsay. I blink twice.

Is that right? Is my *sister* sitting next to *my* ex—the all-state basketball champion and school heartthrob?

I nudge Hana hard.

"No way," she hisses, seeing them together. "How did she manage that?"

"Whatever she wants, she gets," I say. "Told you. She's not bound by the same rules of physics and popularity like the rest of us."

It's true. Lindsay is a hard-core suck-up, and she's not afraid to do whatever it takes to get into the good graces of the beautiful people. I shouldn't be surprised she zeroed in on Ryan. Lindsay, for her part, does not turn, so I can't catch her eye. She's probably ignoring me on purpose. And she seems to be sitting awfully close to Ryan. I get an unpleasant thought. Does Lindsay like him? It wouldn't be hard to imagine. He is gorgeous. I push the thought out of my head. Surely she doesn't, though. He's my ex. Even Lindsay wouldn't sink that low.

I turn away from her and look at the faculty sitting at the front of the chapel. Headmaster B (that's Charlotte Brontë, for those of you keeping score) is going through her morning announcements. She's saying something about a new rule being established for Bard runaways, and the fact that anyone entering the forest without permission will be pursued by Guardians and tracking dogs. That doesn't sound good. But, since I have no plans to head into the forest (the last time I did that, I ended up right back on the Bard campus anyway), I start to tune out. I glance behind Headmaster B and my eyes follow the familiar line of faculty members: Coach H (Hemingway), Ms. W (Woolf), and even Mr. B (Blake). It hits me suddenly that they all look a little world-weary, and I guess I would be, too, if I was stuck in purgatory for who knows how long, teaching a new crop of misfits every year.

Ms. W told me that all of them have certain tasks to do before they're allowed to leave this plane, but I'm not even sure they know exactly what would help them leave. A number of teachers have gone crazy and tried to leave. Emily Brontë, for example, was willing to destroy the entire school and even the world, just to end her time in purgatory.

My eyes slide to the end of the faculty line and settle on Ms. P. She looks particularly miserable. She seems to be studying a small framed photo in her hand. When she catches me looking at her, she slips the small frame in her pocket and frowns at me. Quickly, I look away. The last thing I need to do is get on Ms. P's bad side. Again.

After announcements at morning assembly, we file out of the campus chapel. While in the crowd, Hana gives me a nudge.

"Uh-oh, don't look now," Hana says next to me. "You aren't going to believe this."

I follow her gaze and I see my sister has cornered Heathcliff. Apparently moving in on my ex-boyfriend wasn't enough excitement for one day. She's got to try to muck up things with my would-be guy. She's prattling on to him about something probably really embarrassing, like my flossing habits, and I can see him shifting his weight and looking a little uncomfortable. Heathcliff is acting like he's gotten his foot caught in a bear trap and doesn't know how to get free.

When I get close enough to them to eavesdrop, I hear the tail end of something seriously mortifying.

". . . And you know she'*th* like, *totally* in love with you. I mean, *th*he writes about you all the time, about how my*th*teriou*th* you are, and how *th*he can't figure you out at all, and—"

"Lindsay!" I shout. I can't believe what my sister is saying. She was born without an edit button. Instantly, I feel my face turn bright red.

"Oh, hey, Miranda. We were just—"

"Lindsay, can I *speak* to you a minute? Alone?"

Lindsay shrugs as if it's no big deal, then peels herself away from Heathcliff and follows me. I whirl on her only when we're far enough from Heathcliff so he can't hear.

"What do you think you're *doing*?"

"Helping along your love life," Lindsay says. "No need to thank me."

"*Thank* you? You have to be joking. You're *ruining* my life!"

"God, Miranda, chill. I'm just telling the boy about your true feeling*th*. I mean, he ha*th* a right to know."

We both glance over at Heathcliff, who still looks a bit dazed, like he's not sure what hit him.

"You don't know anything about boys," I say. "You can't just *tell* them you're in love with them."

"Why not?"

"You just *can't*." I send a worried look to Heathcliff. Lindsay probably just scared him off permanently. Not that there could be anything between us, since the faculty have put him off limits. Still, I'd rather believe that he *wants* to be with me, but can't because of the Bard rules.

I glance down at her feet and am reminded that she's wearing my Steve Maddens.

"Those are *my* shoes!" I cry. "I've told you a *million* times not to wear them!"

Lindsay huffs. "Geez, no need to get all bent out of *th*hape. They're just *th*hoe*th*. And as far as Heathcliff goe*th*, I wa*th* just trying to do you a favor."

"Well, don't. I don't need favors. I have *real* friends, okay? I don't have to do papers for people to get them to like me." This comes out harsher than I intend, and I see Lindsay's face fall just a little.

"You can be a real bitch sometimes, you know that?" Lindsay says, hurt, as she turns away from me.

It's true. Guilty as charged. But Lindsay just . . . well, brings out the worst in me.

"Lindsay, wait . . ." I shout and grab her arm. I'm about to apologize, when she whips around, glaring at me.

"Let *go* of me," she nearly shouts, putting all her weight against me as she tugs to get her arm free.

"Is there a problem here, girls?" asks Ms. P, who has materialized from seemingly nowhere. This is because she probably has. Ghosts have a way of creeping up on you.

"There's no problem," I say, releasing Lindsay's arm. She rubs it and gives me a rueful look as if I gave her a serious injury.

"There *ith* a problem," Lindsay says, glaring at me.

"*Tsk tsk,*" Ms. P says, shaking her head. "That means another week of detention for you, then," she tells me.

"But aren't you even going to listen to my side?" I can't believe this.

"No," Ms. P says, shaking her head. "Now, Lindsay, why don't you come with me to my office? I have some extra credit I was going to offer Miranda, but I think you could make better use out of it."

"But, Ms. P . . ."

"Let's go, Lindsay," Ms. P says, gently putting her arm through Lindsay's. She turns to me, a half smile on her face, "And don't forget bathroom duty tomorrow."

As if I could.

Five

There is, honestly, only so much toilet scrubbing a girl can take without starting to seri- ous lose it. Not to mention that I think I'm starting to smell like bleach even when I'm not scrubbing sinks.

"Phew, what is that?" cries Blade, waving her hand in front of her face when I sit down next to her in English class, my first period of the day.

"Don't ask," I say. "I don't suppose you have a spell that could send my little sister into another dimen- sion?"

"No, but I might be able to make her hair fall out," Blade says.

I consider a bald Lindsay. This makes me smile.

The bell tolls outside, signaling the start of class, and Ms. P sweeps into the room, dumping papers on her desk and focusing straight on me.

"So, *Miranda,*" Ms. P says. "Tell me about the central theme of *Moby-Dick.*"

Ms. P has a look on her face that suggests she thinks I haven't read it. Well, *ha,* I did.

"It's about a whale," I say, which causes the whole class to laugh. "But more than that, it's about revenge and obsession."

Ms. P seems momentarily taken aback. "Care to elaborate?"

"Ahab, the captain of the ship, lost his leg to Moby Dick and he's obsessed with finding and killing that whale. He keeps on his mission even when it's clear that he's endangering his whole crew."

"Suck-up!" someone in the back of the class snickers. Ms. P silences him with a look.

"Is that all, Miranda?" she asks me, a look of mild annoyance on her face. It's like she was hoping to catch me off guard, but didn't, and now she's ticked off about it.

"Um, yeah, I mean, that's basically it."

"Well, since you know the book so well, I'm going to assign you and the rest of the class a ten-page essay on obsession," Ms. P says. The entire class groans, and someone throws a paper airplane at the back of my head. Great. I've just become the class's worst enemy, and all because I read the book. "Oh, and Miranda, since you're already so much ahead of the class, I expect your paper on my desk by Thursday."

"Ms. P is not as adjusted as some of us are," Ms. W tells me during our counseling session. "Some of us are resigned to our fates, but others are overcome with regret."

"But why does she want to take it out on me? You don't take things out on the students."

Ms. W puts down her pen and looks at me over her notepad. "Ms P left children behind, and she's never forgiven herself for it," Ms. W says. "I didn't have children, and all I left behind was madness, so I've adjusted to life after death."

I nod. I guess that makes sense. I realize that there's a lot about my teachers I don't know, even though they are famous ghosts.

"But why are some of you here, and some aren't?" I ask. "I haven't met Jane Austen yet."

"We died before we were supposed to die, remember?" Ms. W prompts. "Most of us, like Ms. P and myself, are suicides, but some are accidental deaths. In any case, we've got unfinished business here on Earth."

Ms. W gets a far-off look on her face. She seems sad.

"Aren't you supposed to help me learn to write? Then you can break the cycle and leave?" Last year,

Ms. W said she thought her unfinished business on this plane was helping young authors.

"I honestly don't know if it's that simple," Ms. W says. "I don't know what exactly I'm supposed to do. It's just a guess."

"Well, I want to help." I hate to think of Ms. W stuck here for eternity. She and Coach H are two of the few teachers here who are actually nice to me.

"You've done enough for us—and the school—already," Ms. W says. "You need to focus on living your own life. You shouldn't really be thinking about us, or about death in general. You have a life yet to lead. Speaking of, how's your sister adjusting to life at Bard?"

I pause. I hate it when Ms. W turns the tables on me. She does it so well, that just when I think I'm getting somewhere, she flips the question back to me.

I shrug.

"That well?"

"I dunno," I say, and shrug again. My sister is just one topic of conversation I'm happy to avoid.

"Well, you should keep an eye on her," Ms. W says. "For one thing, she has powers that she doesn't know about."

Lindsay, not being in on the big secret, doesn't know our great-great-great—you get the idea—was a fictional character and that means we've got special powers here in literary purgatory.

"Just make sure she doesn't fall in with the wrong people," Ms. W is saying.

"Who are the *right* people around here?"

Ms. W gives me a sly smile. "You know what I mean," she says. "I've seen her with Parker."

"Yeah, I have, too." I sigh. "It's a problem, no doubt."

I can't believe Parker really *likes* Lindsay, so I can only assume it's part of a greater plan to make my life miserable. It's not good enough for her that Ryan broke up with me and just wants to be friends now. Parker's like Ahab. She's obsessed with revenge.

"You'd better be careful, both of you, this semester," Ms. W says. "Your father gave the entire faculty strict instructions. If either one of you gets into any serious trouble while you're here, then you're both headed to juvenile detention."

"He's always threatening to do that," I say.

"I think he's serious this time," Ms. W says. "And anyway, it's probably a good idea to keep an eye on your sister. If she's anything like you, she's a magnet for trouble."

"Uh, thanks," I say sarcastically.

"I'm just being honest with you," Ms. W says, her eyes flashing with humor. There's a lot she thinks but doesn't say. "Speaking of honesty, how are you and Heathcliff getting along?"

"Fine," I say. Absently, I fidget with the locket around my neck. *His* locket.

"You know you can't get too close to him," Ms. W warns me. Then again, Ms. W never took a liking to Heathcliff. She's been trying to warn me to stay away from him since he first appeared on campus.

"I know," I say.

"And we're serious about the no romantic contact rule," she adds.

I nod. "I *know* already."

"Well, just as long as you also know there's a difference between knowledge and action. Just watch yourself. Because there are worse things out there than juvenile detention."

"You're saying Heathcliff is worse than jail?"

"I'm saying be careful, that's all," Ms. W says.

After our counseling session, I step out onto the commons, and see Heathcliff sitting under a tree. He's trying to read *Moby-Dick* and doesn't seem to be having much luck. His brow is furrowed in frustration, and while I watch, he gives up, throwing the book on the grass and crossing his arms across his chest. This reminds me that Heathcliff only recently learned to read, and that last year I promised to help tutor him, but never managed to find time.

I pause, hesitant to approach him since Lindsay told

him God-knows-what embarrassing details about me. But then he catches me looking at him, and he gives me a half smile. My heart speeds up a little, and I decide to just pretend the Lindsay incident never happened.

"That's a tough book to read," I say, walking up to him and taking a seat beside him in the grass. I pick up the wayward copy of *Moby-Dick* and absently flip through the pages. "I barely finished it myself."

Heathcliff glances over at me, but doesn't say anything. His dark, curly hair is unruly as usual, and he's wearing his trademark scowl. The Bard Academy uniform for boys—a white shirt, Bard blazer, and navy pants—does nothing to soften his rough edges. He's also got a bit of stubble, which never seems to go away no matter what time of day it is.

"Reading seems like a waste of time," he tells me, speaking at last.

I nod. "It can be, I guess, but not always," I say. "Besides, what are you going to do if you flunk out? The teachers would probably use it as an excuse to send you back to *Wuthering Heights*."

"What if I can't go back? There's only a bit of the book left. We don't even know if it still works."

"Do you really want to take that chance?" I ask him.

Heathcliff frowns. "I guess not."

"But I could help you," I say. "Tutor you, if you want. I mean, you can do this. If you put your mind to it."

Heathcliff glances up at me and gives me a long, deliberate look. I can't tell what he's thinking, as usual. Still, there's something so magnetic about his dark brown eyes. I don't know what it is, but they suck me in every time, and I just can't look away. It's like he sees straight through me.

"I'd like that," he says, and he gives me a little smile.

"Great," I say, and smile back.

I move closer to Heathcliff and open the book so that we can both read it. Our arms are touching, and I can feel the warmth of him through my sleeve. I glance around the commons to see if there is any faculty about, but I don't see any. And besides, we aren't making out. We're studying, and that's not against the rules.

Sitting so close to him, it's hard to believe he's a fictional character and not *real*. That he could disappear back to another place at any time. I'm hyperaware of his every move, from when he shifts his arm next to mine to the slight bend of his head.

I start by reading some of the book aloud, but when I glance up, I notice that Heathcliff isn't reading along with me, he's just staring at me.

"Your hair is different," he says to me, pushing a bit of it out of my face with his finger. "It's longer."

I'd been letting it grow over the summer, but I only really think I managed to get an inch and a half or so. I'm surprised he noticed. Boys usually don't see small details.

"Do you like it?"

"Yeah," he says, and nods. "It reminds me of . . ." Abruptly, he trails off. We both know he's talking about Catherine Earnshaw, my great-great-great-great-grandmother, and Heathcliff's true love. When we first met, he thought I looked so much like Catherine that he called me Cathy.

"Do you miss her?" I ask him, wanting him to say no. After all, it's hard to compete with somebody's soul mate.

Heathcliff just stares off across campus and doesn't respond. I guess I've gotten too personal. I glance up and see Ryan walking with Parker across the commons toward the library. Parker catches me looking, and tucks her arm in his. They're framed by the old limestone buildings on campus and they look like the picture-perfect couple posing for some kind of boarding school catalog.

They have a shared history—Parker was once best friends with Ryan's ex-girlfriend, Rebecca, the one that died in the car crash two years ago. That's what got Ryan sent to Bard in the first place. He was the one driving, and it was rumored he had been drinking, even though he passed a Breathalyzer.

I don't know the whole story because Rebecca is just a subject Ryan never talks about. To me, at least. Apparently, he talks about it with Parker a lot, according to her. I don't know why he never felt comfortable confiding in me. Parker once told me it was because Ryan was still in love with Rebecca. I wonder if I'll ever know.

My stomach tightens. I wish I didn't care about him at all. I wonder if I can stand watching Parker put her moves on him.

Heathcliff sees me staring at Ryan and frowns.

"Do *you* miss *him*?" he asks me.

Touché. "I . . ." I pause. I guess I don't know the answer to that question.

"Forget it," Heathcliff says, peeved, gathering up his books and standing.

"But, wait . . . I just started the reading lesson," I stammer stupidly.

"The lesson's over for today," Heathcliff says, storm clouds again darkening his features, his tone leaving no room for argument. Before I can say more, he's turned and left me alone on the lawn.

Six

"So you've got boy troubles? What *else* is new?" Blade asks me, shrugging. She, Hana, and I are all sitting together at dinner, pushing around unrecognizable mush on our plates. The cafeteria is dark and gloomy as usual, just like most of the rooms on campus. The lights above are dimly lit chandeliers with flickering bulbs. They give off about as much light as candles, and the ancient electrical wiring, always patchy at best, gives off little surges now and again.

The walls are all dark-paneled wood and the room is filled with long, wooden tables paired with benches that are bolted to the floor. All the furniture at Bard is bolted down, to prevent kids from stealing or throwing it.

"I don't know why you're getting so worked up about Heathcliff, anyway," Blade says. "You know he's only going to be here for another two years."

Blade's referring to the fact that Heathcliff has a three-year absence from *Wuthering Heights* and he's already spent a year of it here. The faculty said he has to return after that period to keep the fictional world stable.

"Thanks for reminding me," I say, fingering the locket around my neck. "And I can't help it. There's just something about him."

"Are you girls pining over me again?" Samir asks, appearing with his tray and scooting in next to Hana. "You know, I'm always available for a quickie."

"Shut up, Samir," Hana says, giving him a nudge.

"Well, I've got something that will interest you," he says, tossing a copy of the school paper down on the table. "It's fresh from the presses."

I look down at the headline, and see a story on the front page claiming that Robert Louis Stevenson based part of his book *Treasure Island* on Bard Academy's Shipwreck Island. Apparently he visited it briefly during a trip to the United States. He found the legends about pirate treasure hidden at Whale Cove so fascinating that he decided to write about it.

"It says here that there might be 'real buried treasure' on this island," Samir says. "If we found it, we could be rich."

"You're already rich," Hana reminds him. Samir does come from a wealthy family, although his traditional Indian mother has arranged marriage in mind for him when he turns nineteen. His refusing to even consider marriage is what got him sent to Bard in the first place.

"Yeah, but I'm going to be written out of the will after what I pulled," Samir says. "I should just run away now and save myself a lot of grief later."

"I'd say pirates and buried treasure are definitely something the LITs should investigate," Blade adds. The LITs—Literary Investigation Team—is something Blade invented last semester for our little circle. She even had T-shirts made, although none of us wear them.

"Why should the LITs, er, I mean, we, investigate pirates?" I ask. "They're not literary."

"Sure they are," Samir says. "What about *Treasure Island*? That's literary."

I'm only half listening to the discussion about pirates and buried treasure. I'm scanning the cafeteria for any sign of Heathcliff. I want to apologize, or something, I don't know. I see him hanging at the edge of the cafeteria line, grabbing a mystery dinner. I'm plotting how to get his attention when loud peals of laughter from the other side of the room grab my attention. It's Parker Rodham's table. The table is full of rich kids and her clones—girls who follow her around and worship her. Normally, I try to avoid that area of the cafeteria altogether, especially since Ryan has been known to sit there on occasion. But now they're being so loud that it's impossible not to look.

Ryan is, as I guessed, sitting next to Parker. Parker, in turn, has ordered one of her clones to get up on the table.

The clone scrambles up, standing tall, wearing her Bard Academy uniform just like Parker Rodham's (skirt cut three inches shorter, white leggings that go down to midcalf, and blouse unbuttoned low enough to reveal cleavage). She's got her hair dyed exactly the same color as Parker's, and wearing the same high ponytail and the same too-dark eye shadow and glossy lips. But there's something about *this* clone, though, that looks strangely familiar. Too familiar.

With sinking horror, it dawns on me that the clone is not just any Parker clone, *that* girl is my sister.

"Oh my *God*," I manage to squeak, even as it feels like someone has kicked me in the stomach. My sister has gotten a Parker Rodham makeover! My sister is now officially a Parker clone, slave to the girl I call my mortal enemy.

"Hey, isn't that . . . ?" Blade says.

"It sure looks like . . ." Hana says.

"Your sister!" Samir finishes.

"Do it! Do it! Do it!" the table starts chanting to Lindsay, banging their fists on the top so loudly that they bounce plates and silverware. Ryan, I notice, is the only one not chanting. He's got a worried look on his face.

Just then, my sister starts belting out "Yankee Doodle Dandy" while doing high kicks on the table. Food and dishes fly everywhere, even as Parker and her cronies start laughing hysterically. Lindsay, only encouraged by their attention, acts even more outrageous, and starts doing her own version of the cancan, not caring that Parker is laughing *at* her and not *with* her. Or that she is showing half the school her underwear. I glance over at Heathcliff, who is watching the whole scene with a disapproving scowl. Heathcliff is no fan of Parker, and he's no fan of anyone who'd make a fool of themselves to try to impress her. After a minute, he turns, disgusted, and leaves the cafeteria.

I don't think I've ever been so embarrassed in my entire life.

"She's going to get in trouble," Hana says, worried. She nods to the Guardians—Bard's versions of mall security—at the corners of the cafeteria. They're starting to take notice of the ruckus. If she doesn't quit, and soon, Lindsay is going to have a one-way trip to the headmaster's office. I remember what Ms. W told me about my dad's threats to send us to juvie if either of us gets in trouble. I've got to stop her.

"Lindsay!" I shout, jumping up and heading toward

her. I reach her before the Guardians do, and nearly have to step over Ryan to get to her. I ignore him for now, even as I feel him looking straight at me. I have bigger problems at the moment.

"Lindsay, you're going to get in trouble, *stop* it," I tell her, pulling on her wrist. "Get down, *now*."

"Leave me alone," she barks at me.

And then, a wayward gravy-drenched roll hits me in the face and tumbles down my chest, leaving an oily smudge down the front of my Bard Academy uniform. Parker, or one of her clones, threw it.

"Booo!" they hiss at me.

"Guys! Cut it out," Ryan says, annoyed. He stands and holds out his hand. "Lindsay, come on, that's enough."

She looks at him and smiles, and then hops off the table and back into her seat. The Guardians stop their forward momentum, resuming their posts at the edges of the tables. Crisis averted—for now. I wipe congealed gravy from my forehead and flick it on the ground.

"Miranda . . ." Ryan lifts up his hand as if to help me. But what can he do? Besides, this isn't exactly how I pictured our first conversation since the "let's be friends" speech last semester. I never imagined that the first time he'd see me close up again I'd be covered in gravy. My face feels hot, and if that's not enough, I feel hot tears prick at my eyes. Don't cry. Do *not* cry, I order myself. I pray the floor opens up and swallows me whole. It's Bard. It could happen.

But it doesn't.

"Forget it," I say, wiping more gravy off my face and turning away from the table. As I walk away, I hear Parker tell Ryan, "Let the little baby go cry it out," and it's all I can do not to burst into tears right there.

Seven

"I will so put a hex on Parker," Blade tells me the next day in study hall.

"What about my sister?"

"Her, too, if you want," Blade says. "All I need is some of their hair, some chicken livers, and garlic powder."

"Oooh, I love garlic, what are we making?" Samir asks, sliding into the seat next to Blade.

"We're making curses," I say.

"Hexes, technically," Blade tells him.

"What's the difference?" Samir asks.

"For one, you need liver, for the other, chicken blood," Blade says.

"Sorry I asked," Samir says, wrinkling his nose.

"I just can't believe my sister is a Parker clone," I say, shaking my head. "That girl can never think for herself."

"Maybe it's just a phase," Blade says. "Like when I was once a prep for a week."

"*You* were a prep for a week?" Samir asks, amazed.

"Yeah, there are lots of things you don't know about me," Blade says and winks at him. Blade, who once had a crush on Samir, seems to be taking an interest again. Hana won't be happy about that. She's had a secret crush on Samir since I've known her. Of course, it's so secret that she won't even admit it to me.

Before I can ponder this further, outside the main bell tower tolls three times in short bursts.

"What was that? Is study hall over already?"

"No, that's the signal that someone's run away again," Blade says. "They just started ringing the bell when it happens, or so I heard. Then they send Kujo after them."

Outside a nearby window we see Guardians scramble toward the woods, as if looking for someone. They all have dogs on leashes. At the head of the pack is Coach H.

"What's he doing with the goon squad?" Blade asks.

"He must've done something to tick off Headmaster B," Samir says. "But why do they even need the search-and-rescue team? I thought it was impossible to escape from this place."

"It is," I say, thinking back to when I tried to run

away my first night at Bard a year ago. I got lost in the woods and then ended up circling right back to campus like I'd never left. The woods were definitely a spooky place, and nearly impossible to find your way in or out of.

"Maybe they're not trying to prevent them from running away," Blade says. "Maybe they're trying to protect them from what's *in* the forest."

Samir looks at me, and I look back. We're both remembering that last year William Blake's tiger was on the loose in the forest. That was not a good semester.

"What do you know that you're not telling us?" Samir demands, turning to Blade. He looks worried. He is not the bravest of our little circle of friends. "If that tiger is back, I'm transferring, I swear to God."

"No tiger," Blade says. "Some of my friends said they saw some dudes hanging out in the forest."

"Dudes?"

"Yeah, dudes, with long hair. I dunno. They didn't get a good look at 'em." Blade shrugs. Very little scares Blade.

"I guess that's slightly better than a tiger," Samir says. "So I *guess* I'm not transferring." He pauses. "Yet," he adds.

"Well, maybe we should investigate," Blade says. "This sounds like a case for the LITs."

"Man, you are *really* pushing the LITs this semester," Samir says, shaking his head.

"What? I'm just waiting for it to catch on."

"Well, keep waiting," Samir says. "I don't understand why everything that happens on this campus is always *our* problem. Why can't someone else battle whatever crazy fictional disaster is on the loose *this* time?"

"You're overlooking the fact that not everything at this school happens for a supernatural reason," I say, watching as Parker enters the library, followed by two of her clones, and my sister. Parker orders my sister off to get some books for her. Lindsay happily trots off to the research section. She's already writing Parker's papers, no doubt. The thought makes me want to break something.

"Sometimes there's a reasonable explanation," Samir adds.

"Yes, like Parker Rodham," I say, a sinking feeling in my stomach. Parker is planning something evil for Lindsay. I just don't know what.

For the next several days, I see plenty of Lindsay. I see her fetching Parker's books. I see her cleaning off Parker's tray in the cafeteria. I see her scrambling to pick up anything Parker accidentally drops. And Parker always manages to send me a nice, smug smile, to be sure that I know that *she* knows this is driving me crazy.

Of course, Lindsay won't listen to reason. In fact, she won't listen to me at all. I catch her as she's heading out of homeroom one morning. We're standing in Austen Hall, between rows of lockers, as students mill past us.

I decide to get right to the point.

"Lindsay, you have to be careful with Parker. She's a backstabber and can't be trusted."

"Whatever. You're just jealous." I notice she's not lisping. I wonder if Parker told her to lose the retainer.

"Of what?"

"Maybe the fact that I'm more popular at this school than you and I've only been here five minutes but you've been here forever. I mean, it's so obvious," Lindsay says.

I sigh. "Parker is evil, Lindsay. She's probably just befriending you to get to me somehow."

"Oh, and you don't think she could just *like me for me*?" Lindsay's eyes are flashing now. She's seriously ticked.

"No, I mean, of course she would," I lie. There's no way in hell Parker would go for Lindsay. She doesn't befriend people in general as a rule. She ruins their lives. Stomps on them like ants. While I'm thinking of how to explain this so Lindsay will get it, I happen to glance down and look at the books in Lindsay's arms. Her spiral notebook is sitting on top, and there's a giant doodle on it in marker. It's a heart and in it is "L.T. + R.K. 4eva." My heart starts to race. R.K.? Ryan Kent?

I grab the notebook.

"Is this *Ryan*?" I say, pointing angrily to the R.K. "Are you crushing on *my* Ryan?"

Lindsay's eyes widen a little, a guilty look flitting across her face, and then she grabs the notebook back.

"He's not *your* anything. You broke up with him," she says.

"Not true," I say. Technically, I broke up first, but then he broke up second. "Besides, you *cannot* like him. You just can't." I am angrier than I should be. But, objectively, there are a million reasons why this won't work. One, Parker would kill her if she found out. And two, hello—he's *my* ex. Sisters cannot date each other's exes. It's a rule. Somewhere. Definitely in stone.

"It's *my* life," Lindsay says, flipping her Parker ponytail. "I can like who I want." And with that, she pushes past me, pressing her "Lindsay loves Ryan" notebook tightly to her chest.

This time, I will kill her. I swear.

Eight

"Ryan won't go for her," Blade tells me with certainty. She and Hana and I are standing outside the cafeteria after dinner.

"She's *way* too young," Hana agrees.

"She's way too something," I agree. I still get a bitter taste in my mouth anytime I think about Lindsay and that stupid notebook of hers. Ryan is objectively gorgeous, but Lindsay's my sister and she ought to show a shred of loyalty. Borrowing (read: stealing) my shoes is one thing. Stealing my ex is in a whole other league, even for Lindsay.

"Anyway, forget them," Blade adds.

"Yeah, forget them, and come to the pit with us," Hana says.

The pit is a giant stone circle at the center of campus in front of the chapel. Every night, there's a lit fire. There are stone benches around it, and it's too dark to study. The only other gathering places are the library and the dining hall, and both of them are heavily monitored by Bard faculty and Guardians. The pit is monitored, too, just more at a distance.

There's not much to do at Bard. There are no computers or televisions or mobile phones, so the pit is pretty much it in terms of excitement. Unless you just want to sit around and count the gargoyles hanging off the eaves on buildings around here (so far, I've counted ninety-three), then the pit is it.

"I don't know," I say, hesitating. Hana and Blade have been trying to get me to go to the pit since the start of school. The pit also is the place you go when you want to see and be seen. I used to hang out there a lot when I was dating Ryan. The idea of going there sans Ryan just makes me feel like a loser.

"Plus, we're juniors now, so we get the *comfortable* benches," Hana reminds me. Technically, all the benches are made of stone, but the ones closest to the fire are unofficially officially reserved for upperclassmen. It can get cold at night, even during warm days at Bard, and the cold stone benches suck the heat right out of you.

"Miranda got to sit on the comfortable benches with Ryan last year, remember?" Blade says. Swiftly, Hana pokes her for reminding me. Not that I could forget. Ryan—a year older than me—would always save me a place next to him, and when I'd sit down, he'd wrap me up in his letterman jacket and keep me warm.

"I just don't think I feel like it," I say, hesitating.

"Come on. You can't avoid Ryan forever," Blade tells me, practically. "Besides, if you keep hiding, then Parker wins."

"Yeah," Hana agrees. "You've got to show her you're totally over Ryan." She pauses, giving me a doubtful look. "You *are* over him, aren't you?"

"Yeah, of course," I say, with more conviction than I feel.

"Good. Then we're going," Blade says, dragging me by the arm.

When we hit the pit, it's packed, as I expected. It's after dinner, and we only have one free hour before curfew, when we have to head back to our dorms for mandatory study time. Everything at Bard is very strict and regulated, so you don't have a lot of free time. The school's motto is "I wasted time, and now doth time waste me." Naturally, it's a quote from Shakespeare, and it's engraved in the campus chapel.

I glance around, but there's no sign of Ryan, Parker, or Lindsay, so I relax a little. Maybe this was a good idea. Maybe I was overacting.

Hana and Blade take one of the last semi-empty up-perclassmen benches, and I crowd in next to them.

The fire pops and cracks, and the smell of wood burning reminds me of a ski vacation we took once back before my parents got divorced. We spent a week in Colorado, and Lindsay first learned how to ski and I helped her learn. That was back in the days when we got along. I remember a fire that smelled like this one, and drinking lots of hot chocolate, and me telling Lindsay knock-knock jokes, and Lindsay pretending they were funny. My parents barely even fought the whole week. It was a good trip.

I wonder what happened to us. To Lindsay. To my parents. To me. How do you go from happy to totally dysfunctional in a few years?

Oh yeah, your dad runs off with his secretary and totally abandons the family. Yeah, that's how it happens. Then he divorces said secretary and marries *another* one. Dad can never find grass green enough. And then my sister is the only one who is okay with my dad being a cheater and my mom being a doormat, so my parents start treating her like a princess and me like a pariah because I tell the truth and they don't like it.

Dad's faults are obvious—he pretty much wears them on his Brooks Brothers shirts. But Mom's are a little more subtle. Until she started dating Mr. Perkins, I think she was still hoping Dad would take her back. She's a pleaser, Mom. Always wanting other people to like her. Come to think of it, Lindsay is a lot like Mom. Desperately craving approval all the time.

Since Lindsay is like Mom, I wonder if that makes me like Dad? God, I hope not. Dad is the last person on earth I want to be like.

Still, I wonder if Lindsay is my fault somehow. Did I fail her, like Dad failed us?

As if I conjured Lindsay by thinking about her, she appears at the outer ring of the pit. I smile at her, and I'm about to wave her over, thinking maybe I shouldn't be so hard on her, when Parker and the rest of her clones appear next to her. Parker sees me straight away, and then leans over and whispers into Lindsay's ear. I know without hearing what she's saying that this is not going to be good.

"Miranda," Lindsay barks at me, walking over toward our bench. "That's *Parker's* seat. So you guys have to move."

Lindsay is wearing her hair just like Parker's in a high ponytail, and she's got on Parker's perfume, too. It smells like she bathed in it. It's making my eyes water.

Blade's eyes narrow and Hana stiffens next to me. I can tell that Blade wants to stay and fight and Hana wants to flee. I'm somewhere in the middle, but one thing is for sure, I'm not going to let my little sister boss me around.

"Tell Parker that if she wants this bench, she has to come over here herself." I'm tired of my sister playing errand girl for Parker the Evil. If Parker wants to fight, then she ought to at least do it herself.

Before Lindsay can relay the message, Ryan suddenly appears at her elbow.

"Is there a problem here?" Ryan asks. Great, now my ex is joining in on the fun. Throw in a bit where I'm naked and forgot to study for a final exam and this is my worst nightmare.

"Yeah, *Miranda* won't move," Lindsay says, crossing her arms. "*Tell* her that's Parker's bench." She leans over just enough so Ryan can get a look at her cleavage. Is my sister *flirting* with my ex? Oh, I had better *not* be seeing this.

"I don't see her name on it," Blade scoffs, making a big show of looking for an engraving.

"We can sit somewhere else," Ryan says quickly. "It's no big deal."

"But it *is*," Lindsay says, stomping her foot. "The only benches left are the cold ones."

Then Ryan does something that takes me by surprise. He throws his arm around Lindsay's shoulders and pulls in close enough to whisper something in her ear. Her eyes get big and bright.

I feel a twinge in my stomach. Jealousy? What is Ryan doing getting so cozy with my sister?

"Seriously?" Lindsay says when he's finished. "You mean it?"

"Sure do," Ryan says, and then he hands her his letterman jacket. The very same jacket that I wore most of last semester. She giggles and puts it on and gives me a look that says "Ha!" and she then trots happily back to the other benches. I can't believe what I've just seen. Is Ryan going after my *sister*? I feel hot and then cold and then hot again. "Furious" is the word that comes to mind. F-U-R-I-O-U-S.

I glance quickly over the fire and see that I'm not the only one. Parker's mouth is pressed in a thin line. She's only barely keeping it together, and I'm sure it's only for Ryan's benefit. She gives Lindsay a stare that would kill a weaker person, but Lindsay doesn't even register it, because she's patting the letterman jacket like it's a puppy dog. Oh, she is in for a world of pain, and not from me. Parker may have been out to humiliate me before, but now she's gunning for Lindsay.

"Sorry, guys," Ryan says, flashing us an innocent smile, completely oblivious to the fact that he's just started World War III.

"Keep your friend Parker on a leash," Blade tells him.

"She won't bother you again," Ryan promises, but he's looking at me. I'm too mad to even respond, so all I do is nod curtly and look away. That's when I see

Heathcliff standing very still under a tree a little distance from the pit. He's watching me closely. It's the first time I've seen him since my sister went Broadway in the cafeteria, and the first time we've made eye contact since he ran off and left me on the commons after thinking I still had a thing for Ryan. And now he sees me talking to Ryan? Not good. Not good at all.

I put up my hand in a little wave, but Heathcliff just shoves his hands in his pockets and walks quickly in the other direction.

It's official. My life should be declared a national disaster.

Nine

The next day, I look for Heathcliff everywhere, but can't find him. I feel like I need to explain.

"Have you guys seen Heathcliff?" I ask Blade, Hana, and Samir, who are gathered for what they call dinner in the cafeteria. We've just finished eating and we're piling our trays on the conveyer belts near the exits.

"Not since fifth period," Blade says. "And he seemed to be in one of his moods."

"I don't think he has moods. I think he just has one mood," Hana says.

"Yeah, royally pissed off," Samir adds.

"He's not surly all the time," I say, thinking about the afternoon on the commons. He definitely smiled at me then.

The three of them give me skeptical glances as we push through the doors and head outside. "Oh yeah, he's only surly *when he breathes,* that's all," Blade says.

"You think he frowns in his sleep?" Hana asks.

"If he even sleeps at all," Samir says. "Do fictional characters need to sleep? He certainly doesn't seem to need to eat, since he's skipped most of the cafeteria meals around here."

"He does need to eat, and I'm sure he needs to sleep," I say. "He's just like us."

"Yeah, only he's actually a figment of somebody's imagination," Hana points out.

"Does that mean I'm a figment, too?" I ask.

"No, you're only one-sixteenth a figment," Blade says.

"Or is it one-twenty seventh?" Hana asks.

"Hey, guys, look," Blade says, pointing to a new bulletin board outside the cafeteria. Over the top, bold letters read: REWARD FOR INFORMATION. Below it, there's one photograph of a Bard student in a Bard blazer.

"You think that's the runaway?" Hana asks.

"Looks like it," Samir says. "Or, could be anything. What kind of information are they looking for? I could tell them that this guy needs a haircut. You think that's good for cash?"

It's true that the Bard student in the poster has a shaggy mane of blond hair, like a skater.

I make a move toward the board, but my forward momentum is stopped by a hand on my wrist. I glance back and see Heathcliff standing there in the dusk.

"Where the heck did you come from?" Samir asks him, as he and Hana both look startled to find themselves standing next to Heathcliff, who does seem to be able to materialize just about anywhere he wants to. It doesn't hurt that he seems to know all the secret passageways on campus.

Heathcliff doesn't answer them, he just shrugs.

I always forget how tall he is, and how broad his shoulders are. And his eyes are so dark they're almost black.

"Heathcliff! I've been looking all over—" I don't get to finish my sentence because he cuts into it.

"I've got something to show you," he tells me.

"Come on, guys," Blade says. "I think this is our cue to go."

Heathcliff ignores my friends as they turn down the path that will take them to the library. He is looking at me expectantly, his dark eyes fixed on mine and his hand still firmly around my wrist.

I turn away from Blade, Samir, and Hana, even as they are already several steps from me, and let Heathcliff lead me on a path toward the woods.

His hand slips down, and he laces his fingers through mine.

I guess he isn't mad, after all.

Nervously, I glance around us, but I don't see any sign of faculty members or Guardians, and it's nearly dark. Even if someone did see us, we'd look like two average Bard students in uniform, except for the fact that Heathcliff is so tall and broad. His hand nearly entirely covers mine.

Heathcliff heads straight for the woods.

"But . . ." I start. I think about the "dudes" that Blade's friends saw in the woods. Not to mention, if Guardians catch us, the faculty could have us suspended or worse. They could send the dogs after us.

Then again, Heathcliff is the last person to worry about rules. He makes his own.

"Trust me," Heathcliff whispers, and it's all the assurance I need as I let him lead me into the dark path between the trees.

Somehow, being with him, I don't fear getting caught, by Guardians or by whatever we might find in the woods. In general, being with Heathcliff makes me feel safe, probably because he's more dangerous than whatever we're going to run into out here.

Heathcliff doesn't say a word, he just keeps his hand closed tightly over mine, leading me deeper into the woods. He walks as if he knows where he's going, and he even seems to know instinctively where the low-lying tree branches are, and how to avoid walking on tree stumps.

Above the tree tops, the moon is rising. It's big and full and sheds a silvery glow on everything.

I want to say something, ask Heathcliff where we're going, but it just doesn't seem right to talk.

Suddenly, we reach a clearing not too far from where we entered the woods, and there's a small pond there. Heathcliff stops, and when I look up at him, he just puts a finger to his lips.

I glance over at the still, mirrored top of the pond, reflecting the trees and the bright moon above our heads and wait. It's gorgeous, no doubt. I don't think I've ever seen anything so peaceful.

While I'm looking at the pond, a few sparks of light appear. And then a few more.

Fireflies.

They skid over the lake, flashing their bright yellow lights. It starts with a few, and before I know it, there are not just dozens, but hundreds of them, all dancing over the surface of the pond. Tiny, flashing points of light flying above the water and reflected within.

"It's beautiful," I say in a whisper, leaning closer to Heathcliff.

This is what makes him so hard to figure out. He's known for getting into fights and for his merciless seeking of revenge in *Wuthering Heights,* but he's also got a sensitive side, too. He's nothing if not complicated.

I look up and study Heathcliff's face as he watches the fireflies. The silver moonlight glints on his dark curly hair. His dark eyes, as usual, are unreadable. He looks down at me, holding my gaze for a long time. He doesn't seem like a fictional character. He seems very *real*.

I remember the last time we were this close. We were in a secret passageway last semester, and Heathcliff kissed me. I remember his lips, warm and sure, and the taste of him. Salty.

I want him closer. So very much closer.

Before even thinking about the repercussions, I grab the collar of his Bard blazer and pull him closer, and he turns to me as if it were the most natural thing in the world, and then we're kissing, and it's everything I remembered and more.

Ten

As Heathcliff pulls me close to him, hard against his chest, faint alarm bells in the back of my head are going off, the ones reminding me that should we be caught kissing, Heathcliff will be banished from Bard forever. While I know I should pull away, I can't. I've literally turned into jelly. Heathcliff puts his hand on the back of my neck, and then trails the other one down my back. My knees buckle a little and then Heathcliff pulls me even closer to his chest and deepens the kiss.

I know I should stop, but I don't want to. I want this to last forever. No one should smell and taste this good.

It's Heathcliff who pulls away first. I feel a rush of cold air on my face as he pulls away from me, and my eyes flutter open, surprised. Why did he stop?

I try to read his expression in the dark, but he's

got his head turned away from me. And that's when I hear it.

A small branch breaking. Someone or something is walking near us. Maybe ten or twelve feet away.

I stiffen.

Heathcliff puts his finger to his lips to tell me to be quiet, and then he pulls me closer to his chest and shifts a little, so that there's a large oak tree between us and whatever is moving around. He's got my back to the tree and is peering over my shoulder.

I hear another couple of steps, and I can't help myself, I turn to look. In the moonlight, I see that it's a person, although I can't tell if it's a student or a Guardian. I whip my head back around and flatten myself to the tree. Heathcliff pushes himself against me, his entire body tense.

I suddenly realize that should we be found out here, it would be mandatory expulsion for Heathcliff. Even if we tried to tell them nothing was happening between us, I doubt they'd believe us.

We listen as the footsteps fade, and I start to think things are probably fine, and I make a move toward the campus, but Heathcliff restrains me. I glance at him and he shakes his head slowly from side to side.

That's when I hear more footsteps. A second person. I peek around the tree and clearly see it's a man, but he's no Guardian. Or teacher, either. He looks a lot like a pirate. He's got a handkerchief tied around his head and he's wearing threadbare clothes, pants cut off at the knees, and no shoes. Are these the guys Blade's friends saw? They don't look like they belong in this century. They look like they're extras from the set of *Pirates of the Caribbean*. I suddenly remember Samir talking about pirate treasure on the island. Does that mean there are also pirates?

Pirate Man is followed by a second, who is carrying something large slung over his shoulder. It looks like another person. In fact, it looks like a Bard student, a boy. I see white socks and the dark blazer, and a shaggy mop of blond hair. Wait . . . I *know* that kid from somewhere. I strain to get a closer look. Yep. He's the guy in the poster on the bulletin board. The one who supposedly ran away. But he looks like he's not doing any running now. He's definitely being kidnapped.

I try to move away from the tree, but Heathcliff holds me fast. We can't just let crazy men dressed up as pirates take a Bard student.

I nod my head furiously at the men and then at Heathcliff, trying to tell him that we ought to do something, but Heathcliff just shakes his head. I can't believe he's just going to let these guys—whoever they are—kidnap a Bard student. It's clearly what they're doing. We can't just *let* them.

I try to wriggle away from Heathcliff, and in my

haste to do so, my foot lands on a dried branch and it cracks, loudly, beneath my foot. I let out an involuntary "oh" and the footsteps around us stop. They heard me, clearly.

Heathcliff throws his body against mine, crushing me to his chest and muffling my face. Behind me, I hear the footsteps stop, and then more rustling around us. Suddenly, the woods around us seem to come alive with footsteps. Apparently the two guys weren't the only ones in the group. There were more men and they seem to be surrounding us.

Uh-oh. I didn't count on that.

"Run," Heathcliff hisses in my ear, pushing me away from the tree.

I don't need to be told twice.

I take off through the woods, branches whipping at my face as I blindly run toward campus. I hear Heathcliff behind me, thrashing through the brush. There's a crashing sound, and I turn to see Heathcliff in a struggle with what look to be two men. One of them has little or no teeth and his mouth is open in a big O as he chases us. The other is the shirtless guy who has no shoes.

I stop and look around for something heavy to smack one of them with, but even as I do so, Heathcliff quickly gets the upper hand. He smashes the head of one against a nearby tree and then kicks the other in the groin. Both men, dazed and startled, fall to the ground, moaning.

Heathcliff pushes himself away from them and grabs my hand, leading me back toward Bard Academy. I hear footsteps closing in behind us. I don't know how many men there are, but it sounds like a lot. Heathcliff tugs hard on my arm. Up ahead, I can see the lights of campus, and I hear the bell tolling, warning us that it's five minutes until curfew. My legs pump harder, but I still feel like I'm falling behind, and the footsteps behind us are getting closer.

Heathcliff glances back at me and then behind me, a worried look on his face, as we whip through the trees. And then, just as we're five feet from the campus green, Heathcliff yanks my arm hard, swinging me around and in front of him. He's so strong that he catapults me straight through the edge of the trees and onto the landscaped grass. I tumble onto the green, lose my footing, and fall on both knees and my hands, skidding to an ungraceful stop.

I roll over, thinking Heathcliff is going to emerge any second, but all I see is him being pulled back by two sets of hands.

"Heathcliff!"

"Go!" he shouts at me, as he's dragged back into the forest. "Leave me!"

I hear grunts and groans, and what sounds like a scuffle. Then, silence.

"Heathcliff?" I call softly. When he doesn't answer me, I shout louder. "Heathcliff!"

I glance at the line of the woods, frozen to the spot. Should I go back in and look for Heathcliff? Or should I run to get help? And why aren't the men, or whatever they are, coming after me?

After another second, I decide I can't just leave him. I take a step into the tree line, right where Heathcliff disappeared, but I don't see anyone. Everything is quiet. Eerily quiet, as I look from side to side. All I see are tree trunks and tree branches. No sign of Heathcliff or his attackers. And no one is making a sound.

This is dumb. Oh so very dumb. I am so going to regret this.

I step over a tree trunk, and suddenly am caught from behind. A strong hand comes tightly over my mouth.

I squirm and struggle, even as my attacker lifts me easily off the ground, my feet kicking air. In a last-ditch effort, I swing an elbow hard backward, hoping to land in his stomach, which it does, and his grip relaxes a little. I fall forward inches away from the campus lawn and my attacker falls to the ground next to me.

It turns out to be Heathcliff.

He groans and rubs his stomach. "What did you do

that for?" he says, clutching his side and breathing hard.

Glad to see him alive, I throw my arms around him and hug him close. He grunts as I nearly tackle him flat.

"Besides, I thought I told you to go," he says in my ear.

"I guess I'm not very good at following directions," I say, releasing him from my hug. "Are you okay?" I inspect him for damage and notice he's got a small cut above his left eye, and that his knuckles are bleeding.

"Fine, until *you* hit me," he says, wincing as I help him to his feet. We start walking back to my dorm.

"Who were those guys?" I ask him. "They looked like pirates."

"I don't know, but I've seen them around since school started," he says.

"What did they want with a Bard student?"

Heathcliff shrugs. "I don't know."

The bell tower tolls five more times, signaling the fact that I have less than a minute to get to my dorm before curfew. I remember Ms. W warning me about disobeying any Bard rules and the juvie consequences, and I realize I have to go. Heathcliff senses it, too.

"You're safe for now," he says. "They don't come

onto campus grounds, at least not that I've seen. The student must have wandered into the woods."

"I should warn Lindsay, though, just in case," I say. "Make sure she stays clear of the woods."

"Don't worry, I'll do it," Heathcliff says. "You get back to your dorm. Tell Ms. P what's going on."

cara lockwood

Eleven

Despite running all the way to my dorm, I miss curfew by literally a nanosecond. The last bell tolls as I sprint into the door, and come face-to-face with Ms. P.

"You're late," she says, tapping her watch.

"By . . . a . . . second . . ." I wheeze, still trying to catch my breath and putting my hands on my knees. Surely, she's not going to punish me for a second?

"That means an extra week of toilet duty," she says curtly.

"But, Ms. P, that's not fair," I say, straightening. "And besides, it wasn't my fault."

I explain to her about the guys who looked like pirates, and the fact that they were carrying the Bard runaway, and how someone needs to go into the woods after them.

"Just *what* were you doing off campus? And *who*

were you with?" Ms. P asks me. These are not the questions I'm expecting. She doesn't seem too perturbed by the idea of pirates kidnapping Bard students.

"Is that really important? I mean, the pirates or whatever . . ."

"Of *course,* it's important. Anytime you break campus rules it's important."

"Ms. P, punish me later, okay? Can we deal with the bigger problems first? Like kidnapped students?"

Ms. P frowns at me. "Fine," she says. "I'll go now to Headmaster B and see if we can get this sorted out."

She turns to leave me.

"Ms. P?" She doesn't even know how many we saw. She doesn't know all the specifics. "Wait . . ." I say, grabbing her skirt reflexively. As I do, a small picture frame falls out of her pocket. It clatters to the ground in front of me. "Sorry," I say, reaching down to pick it up. I see it's a picture of two small children. Are they hers? The ones she left behind?____

"I'll take that," Ms. P says abruptly, whipping the photograph out of my hand. She scowls at me, and then quickly drops the framed photo into her pocket again.

"Um, so I don't have an extra week of toilet duty?" I ask, hopeful.

"Oh no. You do have toilet duty," Ms. P says, setting her lips in a thin line. "It doesn't matter why you were late, you were still late. And I think I'll add on an extra week since you just admitted to me that you went into the forest. Another Bard rule broken. Now, off to bed! That is, unless you want to add another week?"

Sometimes I really hate Ms. P.

At the top of the stairs, I run straight into Parker Rodham. She's lounging in the hall with two of her clones, blocking the way to my door.

"Miranda, *there* you are," Parker says, her lips curling up into an unfriendly smile. "Broke curfew already. Did Ms. P give you more toilet duty?"

I try to climb over her clones, but instead of letting me pass, the clones spread out even farther, completely blocking the route to my room.

"None of your business," I say.

"*Tsk, tsk, tsk.* Someone's not in a good mood at all," Parker says, pursing her lips. "Is it because of the little friendship that's developed between me and your sister?"

I feel my anger start to simmer and I clench my hands into fists.

"Parker, I don't know what you think you're doing, but if you hurt my sister . . ." I trail off, not quite knowing what I'm threatening to do exactly.

Parker's evil smile only gets bigger. She's clearly not at all intimidated by me. "You'll what?"

"I'll make you regret it," I finish. It sounds lame, but I can't think of anything better. Her clones giggle and whisper to each other.

Parker pulls herself up from the wall, slowly and deliberately, taking a step closer to me so that we're nearly nose to nose. My heart is pounding. I've never actually been in a girl fight before. The closest I've come to fighting is taking a kickboxing class. And I doubt there's room in this hallway to do a good roundhouse.

"I don't think you've got the balls to fight me," Parker says.

"Well, you'd be right there," I say. "I am a girl. Girls don't have balls, but then you might not know that. Didn't you flunk biology last year?"

"I got a C minus," Parker breathes, furious. She's starting to turn red. Academics are not her strong suit, which is probably another reason she keeps Lindsay around.

"Really? That is a surprise." I shared biology with her last semester and her idea of dissecting a frog was to let her lab partner do it while she gave herself a French manicure.

"If I were you, I'd be a little more concerned about your little sister's baby crushes."

"What are you talking about?" I snap.

"In case you haven't noticed, she's completely and pathetically in love with Ryan Kent," Parker practically purrs. She's enjoying this a little too much. I want to punch her. "Ryan thinks it's so sweet, of course, but he's sworn off dating *virgins*. I hear he had a bad time of it with you."

I feel the blush creep up my neck. My face feels like it's on fire. I can't believe Ryan Kent's been blabbing about my virginal status. And to *Parker Rodham,* of all people. This is some twist. Last semester, everyone thought I was the campus whore, and now here Parker is smirking at me because I've not managed to give it up yet. I want to kill them both: Ryan Kent and Parker Rodham. Not necessarily in that order.

"Are you finished?" I ask her, managing to stay calm. It takes every ounce of willpower, but I do it.

"All I'm saying is poor, poor Lindsay. He says he's going to let her down easy," Parker says. I suppose this is why Parker doesn't care that Lindsay has a crush on him. As long as he doesn't reciprocate, I guess it's fine.

I actually feel relieved. *Relieved* that Ryan is going to tell my sister to take a hike. And, yes, this does make me a bad sister. But still, part of me feels like Lindsay is getting what she deserves. You go after your sister's ex, bad things *should* happen to you.

But why am I so happy? It can't just be that Lindsay is getting what was coming to her. I'm happy that Ryan is still single. What does this mean? Just an hour ago, I was kissing Heathcliff, and now I'm happy that Ryan isn't going to make the moves on my sister. I am far beyond confused.

"Good for him," I say, trying to keep my voice neutral, but Parker senses the relief in it. She frowns at me. Part of me wonders—too late—if this whole conversation was designed to test whether I still have feelings for Ryan.

"Oh, and another thing," Parker adds. "I saw you and Heathcliff on the commons tonight. You seemed awfully cozy for a couple that isn't supposed to exist. It would be a shame if Ms. P had to hear about it." She pauses a delicious second and then adds, "Or Ryan."

My heart drops in my stomach. I'm not sure which is worse, the faculty sending Heathcliff off because he overstepped his bounds, or Ryan knowing that I'm making out with Heathcliff.

"You'd better not," I sputter before I can stop myself.

Parker grins. She's got something on me and she knows it.

"So it's Heathcliff you're gagging for?" Parker's lips curl into a slow, evil smile. "Or is it Ryan? Which boy are you going to tease with your virginity? I'm guessing neither one will be interested, once they realize you're not giving it up."

"Shut up, Parker." This goes even deeper than she knows, since I suspect Ryan broke up with me because he couldn't handle the Virginity Thing.

"Who's going to make me?"

"How about me, Barbie Doll?" We both look up to see Blade standing at the end of the hall. "I thought I smelled overpriced perfume," she says, clomping toward us in her Doc Martens.

Instinctively, the clones shrink back from Blade. She is a bit intimidating, what with the nose ring, the black-and-red spiky hair, and her heavy kohl eyeliner. Besides, Parker's clones act like Goth might be contagious. As if letting Blade touch them would instantly turn their fingernails black.

"Anyone want to see a dead rat?" Blade asks, holding up a paper bag. She pretends to toss it at one of the clones, who flinches. "You scared of rat blood? I caught it in the cafeteria. It was eating off our old plates."

The clones look a bit pale. Even Parker seems a tad grossed out.

"It might have rabies, wouldn't that be cool?" Blade asks, swinging the bag closer to the clones. They shrink back and one lets out a little girly squeal.

"Whatever. I'm so done here," Parker says, as if

leaving was her idea. She turns and heads back to her own room. Her clones follow, as if on a string.

"Thanks," I tell Blade after they've gone. "I owe you one." Blade just shrugs.

"Bunch of Barbie Doll wimps," she says, smiling.

"Do you really have a rat in there?" I ask her.

"Are you kidding? I wish," Blade says, opening the bag for me to see. It's full of red Gummi Worms.

"My cousin from home sent a care package," she explains. "She hid candy in hollowed-out books and shipped them off. I have tons of Sour Patch Kids, too, if you like them."

"Thanks," I say. "Maybe later."

"Anytime, my LIT sister," she says, patting me on the back.

Just then, Hana comes out of the bathroom wearing her PJs, with her hair wet. She looks surprised to see us. I guess my confrontation with Parker didn't carry over the shower.

"You're a little late for the action, missy," Blade says.

"What did I miss?" she asks, cocking her head to one side as she swipes her hair with a towel.

"Just about everything," I say.

Twelve

"So who do you think those guys were last night?" Hana asks me, for the hundredth time as we settle in for morning assembly. Ever since I told her about the pirate kidnappers, she's been peppering me with questions. I have the same questions, just no answers.

"I really don't know," I say. "They looked like castaways. Some of them didn't have shoes."

"Great, now we've got shoeless pirate ghosts," Samir says, and sighs. "I swear, I've had it with this school. I'm going to transfer this year. I promise."

"We'll believe it when we see it," Hana says.

"Ditto," Blade agrees. "And you're sure the kidnapped guy is the one from the bulletin board?"

"Positive."

"But what would they want with a Bard student?"

"I have no idea," I say. I glance over a few rows and

see Parker sitting practically on Ryan's lap. Figures. I look over to Parker's clone posse, thinking I'd see Lindsay there, too, but she's nowhere to be found.

Weird. I wonder if this has to do with Ryan telling her he wasn't interested, or worse, Parker sending her off on some crazy errand that will get her into trouble. I have a nagging feeling that something might be wrong. Lindsay would never miss a chance to brownnose the teachers, which is what she does after every morning assembly.

The teachers file into the chapel, taking their places at the front with Headmaster B. Ms. P brings up the rear, and I notice something different about her. It takes me a minute to realize she's smiling. Ms. P never smiles, not about anything, ever. Makes me wonder if she's managed to get a student expelled. That might be the kind of thing she'd be happy about.

"You think it's more fictional characters on the loose?" Samir asks, dragging my attention back to the conversation at hand. He looks a bit worried.

"I wouldn't rule it out," I say. "Who are the famous pirates in literature?"

"There's Long John Silver," Hana says.

"The fried seafood guy?" Blade asks as the music starts, signaling the start of morning assembly.

"No, from *Treasure Island*," Hana corrects, lowering her voice to a whisper as we all stand for the Bard school song. "Robert Louis Stevenson?"

"Sure, whatever," Blade says, pretending to sing but talking instead. "Next you're going to say it's Captain Hook."

"Well, it could be," Hana says. "He's also a fictional character."

"None of the men I saw had a hook for a hand," I say.

Out of the corner of my eye, I see Heathcliff walk in through the side doors, with his dark curly hair a ruffled mess and dark smudges on his Bard uniform. It looks like he hasn't changed from last night's skirmish and he hasn't slept, either. When his eyes find mine across the room he sneaks into our row, just as the music dies down and the students all sit.

I mouth to him "what's up?" silently, since Headmaster B has started her morning announcements.

"It's your sister," he tells me in a forced whisper. "She never came back to her room last night. And when I went out to look for her, I found this in the woods."

He drops a half-torn spiral notebook in my lap. It's Lindsay's. I'd recognize it and her Ryan Kent love declarations anywhere.

I flip open the cover and she's made a few diary entries. They're mostly about how she loves Bard Academy and how it's so much cooler than her old school.

Heathcliff motions for me to skip to the end.

I flip through her chicken-scratch writing and settle on the last page. At the top, it has yesterday's date. She's also drawn a map of the island, and what appears to be a trail to Whale Cove.

She's underlined the last lines on the page three times:

She says if I find Whale Cove, I can have Ryan all to myself. She thinks I can't do it, but I can. I'll find it.

Find what? And who's she talking about? I flip the page, but there's no more after that. I skip backward a page, but her last entry doesn't shed any light on it, either. It's just her talking about how cool Parker's hair is. There's not even a mention of Ryan breaking the news. I wonder if he even got a chance to talk to her.

I glance up and happen to meet Parker's eye. She gives me a smug little smile, and I get the strong feeling she's involved in this somehow. What if Ryan never had any intention of telling Lindsay he wasn't interested? What if Parker, knowing this and being jealous, sent my sister on a wild-goose chase, to make sure she'd be far away from Ryan?

The notebook does say "she thinks I can't do it." Lindsay must be talking about Parker. A dare from

Parker would send Lindsay anywhere, even the forest. And by the look of this map, she was planning on heading all the way to the other side of the island.

The seriousness of this hits me. Lindsay—alone in the forest with pirate kidnappers on the loose—trying to find her way on an island that's really purgatory for a bunch of ghosts, not all of whom are happy to be here. It's a recipe for disaster.

"What's wrong? What is it?" Hana asks me, even as Headmaster B dismisses the students, signaling the end of morning assembly.

My friends lean over and read Lindsay's diary, which is still open in my hands.

"Hey—Whale Cove! Does Lindsay know about the buried treasure?" Samir asks, starting to get excited. But before he can say more, the tower bell rings three times, signaling another missing person. My throat goes dry.

"It's Lindsay," I manage to stutter, even as I try to push my way through the crowd to get outside and to the bulletin board. I don't need to even look. I know I'm right.

"Oh, snap," Samir whispers as my friends see the picture at the same time I do.

It's sitting next to the photo of the first runaway— the blond, shaggy guy. It's Lindsay, before her Parker makeover, with her retainer in and her hair in pigtails.

"So the little sister doesn't fall far from the tree," Ms. P says, coming up behind me.

"What if she didn't run away?" I ask her. "She could've been kidnapped. Even if she did start out on her own, she might not have made it far before—"

"I'm afraid we investigated your reports of, uh, men in the forest," Ms. P says, interrupting me. "And we didn't find anything conclusive. I'm afraid we have to assume Lindsay ran away on her own volition. And in twenty-four hours, if she doesn't return, we'll have to contact your father."

I go stock-still. If Dad knows about this, it'll mean juvenile detention, for the both of us. Because I know Lindsay, and she'll find a way to blame me for all this somehow. That is, *if* Lindsay is okay.

"But what if we find her and bring her back? Before then?" Blade asks, suddenly stepping up from behind me.

Ms. P considers Blade and then the rest of us.

"You know I can't sanction the lot of you going on an expedition," Ms. P says.

"But . . ."

"But nothing," Ms. P says. "Let the faculty sort it out."

"You can't just give us a wink and say you won't report us if we bring back Lindsay with no fuss?" Samir asks.

Ms. P gives him a severe look. "Do I seem like one of those teachers who doesn't mind bending the rules?"

"Um, yeah?" Samir ventures.

"No," Ms. P says. "Students shouldn't explore the island unsupervised, and that includes you. At any time. For any reason."

"We're losing time," Heathcliff says, breaking the silence suddenly. "If we don't look for her now . . ."

"Let us handle it," Ms. P says, more curt than usual, her eyes sharp as she cuts Heathcliff off in midsentence. "And I believe all of you have classes to go to."

Once Ms. P has left, I turn to Heathcliff.

"What did you mean? About losing time?"

Heathcliff meets my gaze, his eyes guarded. "The forest isn't safe for a girl alone," he says.

"You mean the men we saw?"

Heathcliff shrugs. "Among other things," he adds mysteriously, but doesn't elaborate.

"Um, I'm not going to lie to you, you're freaking us out a little," Samir says to Heathcliff, but he just stares at him.

"Do you think you can lead us to her?" I ask Heathcliff.

Heathcliff nods. "I know where Whale Cove is," he says.

"Wait a second, you can't go after her," Samir says. "Ms. P just said . . ."

"I'm in," Hana says.

"And me," Blade adds.

"Have you all gone crazy?" Samir looks at all of us as if we all just sprouted second heads. "I mean, didn't you hear Heathcliff? There are *things* in the forest. Dangerous things, am I right?" Samir glances over at Heathcliff, who nods. "See? He's even agreeing with me. It's not *safe*."

"All the more reason I have to find my sister," I say, determined. "She doesn't know about the island or about the school. She has no idea what she's in for."

"But Ms. P said the faculty was on top of things. They'll find her. They're ghosts. They know everything."

"They don't, actually," Hana adds.

"Well, at least they're already dead," Samir points out.

"Come on—didn't you want to find your buried treasure? Maybe this is your chance," Blade tells Samir. He considers this for a moment and then relents.

"Well, I *guess* it might be okay then. But only if I get eighty percent of what we find."

"How soon do we leave?" I ask.

"Now," Heathcliff says.

Thirteen

Heathcliff gives us just enough time to grab a few supplies from our rooms (snacks, bottled water, and a blanket) and make our way out toward the woods. I also leave a note for Ms. W in my room. I figure if she comes looking for me, she'll find it. I trust her, and am pretty sure she won't call my parents unless she has to, and if we aren't back by the time she comes looking for me tomorrow, then we might need her help.

That is, if we ever leave.

Getting to the woods is easier said than done, since the campus is crawling with Guardians and faculty and it happens to be broad daylight. You don't just walk straight into the woods without attracting some attention. That is, unless you're with the crew team, which practices by the river every afternoon. Hana decides that going separately and meeting up by the river is the best course of action, as one or two of us won't attract as much attention as all five.

I'm supposed to make my way behind the library and into the woods, but before I even round the bend of the library I find myself staring at Parker and Ryan Kent, who are both sitting together on the library steps.

"Miranda," Parker says, looking a little annoyed. I must be mucking up her one-on-one time with the campus' hottest new singleton.

Still, seeing her just makes my blood boil. If it wasn't for her manipulating Lindsay, none of this would've happened.

"I hope you're happy," I tell Parker, getting close enough to her to make her take a step back.

Ryan looks from Parker to me and back again.

"I don't know what you mean," Parker says, trying to look innocent.

"You sent my sister off into the woods," I say through gritted teeth.

"Me? I didn't send your sister anywhere," Parker says, shrugging, as if she couldn't care less about Lindsay. "I have no idea what you're talking about."

"What's wrong? Where's your sister?" Ryan says, cutting into Parker's denial and looking suddenly concerned. "I mean, is she okay?" Ryan looks at me now. He's a little too interested in Lindsay. He sure isn't acting like a guy who's about to tell her he's not looking to date. I glance at Parker, who seems peeved. Maybe Ryan *is* crushing on my sister. Great, that's all I need.

"I think she's gone to Whale Cove, but then Parker knows that already."

Parker just sniffs and rolls her eyes. "Whatever," she hisses under her breath.

"Whale Cove? On the other side of the island? But that's far and . . ." Ryan pauses. "Probably dangerous."

Again, the note of concern. And why do I find that so very annoying?

"I know. That's why I'm going after her." Instead of sounding brave and sisterly, my voice sounds peevish.

"You can't go into the woods. That's against the rules." Parker smirks at me. I realize I've said too much. Now, Parker will head straight to Headmaster B and rat me out.

"I don't care. She's my sister and I have to help her," I say.

"I'm going with you," Ryan says, jumping up from the library steps. Again, he sure is eager to find my sister.

"That's not necessary."

"It is," Ryan says, determined.

"You can't!" Parker exclaims. Because if he goes, she can't tell. She doesn't want to get her golden boy in trouble.

Above my head, the clock tower tolls, signaling the end of free period. That's my sign. I should be in the woods by now.

"You coming or not? I'm late," I say, pulling up the straps of my backpack and heading off in the direction of the woods.

"I'm going," Ryan says, slinging on his backpack.

Parker looks from Ryan to me and back again. "Then I'm going, too."

"You can't go," I say.

"Why not?" Parker says.

"Because this is all your fault," I hiss.

Ryan frowns at Parker.

"She's crazy," Parker tells Ryan. "I have no idea what she's talking about, but Lindsay was my . . . uh, friend." Parker says the word as if it leaves a bad taste in her mouth. "The least I can do is help look for her."

I know Parker is lying. She would rather chew off her own arm than help me or Lindsay. There's only one reason on earth she would be willing to go on this little expedition and that's to keep a close eye on Ryan.

"Look, I've got to go," I say, turning.

"Then we're both going with you," Ryan says as he and Parker follow me.

After narrowly avoiding being caught by two Guardians on patrol, the three of us manage to meet up with the others by the river. As I could've predicted, no one is happy to see Parker.

"What is *she* doing here?" Hana exclaims when I show up with Parker and Ryan in tow.

Heathcliff just looks at Ryan and then at Parker and scowls. His feelings are written all over his face. I feel a pang of guilt. I hadn't thought about how this might hurt Heathcliff. The last person he'd want to deal with is my ex. Not that I had a choice in the matter, but still. Honestly, the last person *I* want to deal with right now is my ex. Especially since he seems to have a thing for my sister.

"Did you also invite the entire marching band?" Samir asks.

"As if I'd be caught dead in the marching band," Parker sniffs.

"It's a long story. Parker and Ryan say they want to help," I say.

"Since when does Parker care about anything but Parker?" Blade asks me, not even bothering to lower her voice.

"I'm right here, you know. I can hear you," Parker says.

"Oh really?" Blade says in mock surprise. "Because I don't care."

The two give each other hostile stares.

Samir takes the opportunity to lean over and whisper in my ear. "Just so you know, I'm still hanging on to my eighty percent of the treasure," he says, face serious. "I'm not splitting it with either of them."

"Um, Miranda? Can I talk to you a minute?" Hana asks me, a worried look on her face. She tugs me aside, out of earshot near a large tree, and whispers, "You know you can't trust Parker. What is she *doing* here?"

"If I'd left her behind she probably would've told on us. At least this way she's an accomplice."

"Yeah, or maybe she just wants to come along so she can kill you and not have to worry about disposing of the body."

"Hana, there are six of us and one of her. I doubt she can kill all of us."

"I'm just saying that we ought to keep an eye on her."

When we return to the group, Heathcliff and Ryan are eyeing each other warily. Heathcliff is slightly taller and definitely broader, but Ryan looks determined not to blink first.

This is so not good. I feel tiny pricks in my stomach, and I realize they're nerves. I don't know what to do— stick close to Heathcliff? Ignore Ryan? My stomach is a tangle of knots. Just when I thought I had it all figured out, that Heathcliff was the one for me, suddenly I'm not so sure. Which one do I like more? I haven't felt this confused since the first day of trig.

After the two boys have their little stare-down contest, Ryan talks first.

"Do you have a problem?" he says to Heathcliff, his voice tight.

Oh no. Don't provoke him, I think. Heathcliff is strong, really strong, and knows how to fight.

Hana sends me a knowing look, as if to say, *see the mess you've made?*

Heathcliff scowls at Ryan, a look that should've scared him, but Ryan holds his ground and doesn't look away. Everyone, even Parker, seems to be holding their breath, waiting for what happens next. Heathcliff is anything but predictable.

I must look worried because Heathcliff glances over at me and holds my gaze for a long second. Then, as if deciding to take the peaceful way out, Heathcliff scoffs at Ryan, as if my ex acting like a tough guy is really funny, and shakes his head. I exhale, relieved. The last thing I want is a fight. But I don't know whether it's because I want to protect Ryan or because I don't want Heathcliff to be the kind of guy who can't control his temper, the kind of bad guy that Ms. W is always warning me about.

Heathcliff meets my eye and then nods toward the forest. I take the cue and follow him.

"Uh, wait, we're going? Already?" Samir asks, fumbling to get his backpack on.

"Come on, slow poke," Blade says, nudging him as she passes by.

"Hang on one second," Ryan says, running up by my side and grabbing me by the elbow. "Heathcliff is leading us?"

"Yeah, why?" I ask Ryan, trying not to get sucked into his blue, blue eyes.

"I mean, you *trust* him? I thought he was a thug," Ryan says, his voice little more than a whisper. I don't know if Heathcliff can hear him or not.

"He's the only one who really knows his way around the forest. We have to trust him."

"But, Miranda . . ." Ryan starts.

Heathcliff, realizing I'm not right behind him, slows and turns and sees that Ryan is holding me up. He doesn't like that one bit. He glares at Ryan. And I'm starting to get annoyed with Ryan, too. I know he doesn't like Heathcliff, but picking a fight with a guy twice his size isn't going to do anyone any good. Is he just suicidal or what?

"I'm following Heathcliff," I say. "If you have a problem with that, then turn back now."

Ryan's face falls a little and, out of the corner of my eye, I see Heathcliff smile smugly. Score one for Heathcliff.

"I'm not going back," Ryan says, clearly not happy about it, but stubbornly keeping to his promise.

Heathcliff leans back and grabs my hand, pulling me forward. I let him, and Ryan doesn't like that too much, either, but he doesn't say anything. He just follows a few steps behind.

Behind us, the bell tolls in rapid succession.

"Um, does that mean what I think it means?" Samir asks us. It sounds like the runaway bell. And that means Guardians will be headed into the woods after us.

"Parker!" Blade shouts. "*You* did this."

"How did I do this?" Parker cries. "I'm *here*, aren't I? Why would I turn myself in?"

Seconds after the bell tolls, I hear dogs in the distance. They're the search dogs and the Guardians won't be far behind.

"Run!" Heathcliff shouts to us, even as the frantic sound of dogs barking grows louder in our ears.

Fourteen

Branches whip at my face, even as I'm sure the dogs are getting closer.

"I hate dogs! Did I mention I hate dogs?" Samir pants behind me.

"Shut up and run!" Blade says, pushing on Samir's back.

"What do you think I'm doing? This *is* me running!" Samir shouts.

"Would you two love birds shut up!" Hana shouts, running past both of them.

Parker and Ryan veer off to the right, just as Heathcliff goes left. He's still holding my hand and I can barely keep up with him. My chest burns and I'm out of breath from running, and it feels like I might throw up. Heathcliff lets go of my hand as the forest gets thicker, and he tries to use both his arms to clear a path for us through the brush.

But pretty soon he's pulling away from me. First a few steps, and then a few yards. I can't even catch my breath enough to tell him to slow down, and before I know it, my foot snags on a branch lying on the ground, and I fall, headfirst, into the forest floor of leaves.

"Miranda!" cries Blade, the closest to me. Hana and Samir, already ahead of us, didn't see me fall.

Blade helps me up. My elbows and knees are throbbing. I'm sure I've done some damage. I don't have time to think about that because suddenly, poking its head out into the clearing, is one of the search dogs. It's huge, and snarling, and it's got drool dripping off its front fangs.

"Nice doggie?" Blade says, putting her hands up. The dog just snarls. "Don't make any sudden movements," Blade tells me. "If it's just the one, we can probably take it."

Two more dogs walk tentatively out of the brush, on our left and right sides. They also have their fangs bared and look like they might pounce at any moment.

"You were saying?" I whisper to Blade.

"I was saying we're totally screwed," Blade says.

I am not a dog person. Not that I have anything against dogs per se, but my family never had one, and so I don't exactly feel comfortable around them. Especially when they're three very ticked-off mutts who look very much like they're going to go for my jugular.

I don't know what kind they are, but they're big, and they're clearly mean, and at any second they're going to jump for us.

Blade and I take a tentative step backward.

"I think we're supposed to put up our hands and make ourselves look bigger," Blade whispers.

"I thought that was for bears and cougars."

"Same difference," Blade says. "Aren't they all carnivores?"

"Wait, these dogs can't be all that bad," I say. "I mean, they're trained to go after Bard students, but surely not eat them, right?"

"Oh yeah, sure," Blade says, nodding. "You want to test that theory?"

"Nice puppy? Nice boy?" I say, offering up my hand to the nearest dog. He just growls and snaps his jaws at me. "Okay, okay—I get the message."

The dog closest to Blade decides to make a move. It leaps in the air, jaws open, eyes mean and wild. Blade throws up her hand to protect her face, and just before the dog reaches her, a flat gray rock hits it in the snout, causing it to fall back, landing on the ground with a whimper.

"What the . . . ?" I say.

A stone whistles by my head and hits the other dog, square in the head, causing it to yelp in pain and bury its snout in its paws. A third stone zigs in and hits the last dog in the stomach. Then there's a hail of rocks and the dogs back off, one by one. Heathcliff walks out of the brush, juggling two more rocks.

"You okay?" he asks me.

"I am now," I say, relief running over me.

"That's animal cruelty," Blade points out. Heathcliff gives her a dirty look. "Not, of course, that I'm complaining, exactly," she's quick to add.

"Hey, uh, guys? Can you give us a hand?" Hana asks. I glance up and she and Samir are hanging precariously from a tree limb a few yards from us. Apparently, they scrambled up to avoid the dogs and now can't quite get down.

Heathcliff helps them down.

"Where are the others?" I ask them when they're safely on the ground.

"Here we are," Ryan says, stepping out of the brush. Parker, who is still winded from running, bends over and puts her hands on her knees.

"I . . . am . . . so . . . going . . . to . . . sue . . . Bard," she sputters, breathing hard. "When my dad finds out about the attack dogs, he's going to have someone's ass on a platter."

"Do they serve ass on platters?" Samir asks, quirking an eyebrow.

"In Parker's family, I'm sure they're silver platters," Blade says. The two of them share a laugh.

Parker frowns at both of them, but they don't seem too perturbed. I notice that Samir and Blade seem to be getting along. And Hana doesn't even seem to mind too much. Hmmm. Interesting.

Heathcliff ignores the banter and focuses on me. "We should go," he tells me, and starts off to the right.

"You sure you want to go that way, tough guy?" Ryan says as Heathcliff passes in front of him. Heathcliff pauses and looks up. He doesn't say anything, just gives Ryan a look like he might squash him like a bug. "*That* way is west," Ryan says, smugly, pointing the direction in which Heathcliff is headed. "And we need to go east. *That* way." Ryan nods in the other direction. "I go camping with my dad a lot," Ryan adds. "I know my way around the woods."

For a second, everyone looks at Heathcliff for an explanation. He sighs, weary of having to explain himself, and annoyed Ryan is questioning him.

"Feel free to follow Ryan," he tells the group. "If you want to run into more dogs."

We all exchange glances.

"You see, they'll be sending more dogs after us, and they'll be able to track us on the ground," Heathcliff says. "But if we cross the White River *that* way," he adds, nodding to the west, "then they'll lose the scent and we'll be free of them. You run into killer tracking dogs much on your little camping trips with Dad?"

Heathcliff can't help but gloat. Ryan turns red.

"Thought not," Heathcliff says, and continues on his way. I follow him, not meeting Ryan's eye.

"I, for one, am for the dog-free path," Samir volunteers, scurrying after us. "You said there's a river? It's not deep, right?"

Heathcliff just glances at him and says nothing.

"I mean, we're talking a stream, here, yeah? Maybe something a little bigger than a puddle?"

After a ten-minute walk, we make it to the banks of the White River. It's apparently a larger branch of the same river the crew team practices on, but this section isn't nearly as calm or as shallow. And it is most definitely *not* a puddle. Or a stream. Try a raging, rapids-filled, roaring river. The surface is churning so quickly it's almost entirely white caps, and it becomes pretty obvious pretty quickly why they call it white.

"No way, nuh-uh," Parker says, shaking her head. "No way are we crossing that."

"Wow, for once I *agree* with Parker," Samir says. "What are the odds? Quick. Someone go buy a Lotto ticket."

"Why don't we go back? We can cross where it isn't so rough," Ryan suggests.

"Be my guest if you want to run into the dogs on your way there," Heathcliff says evenly. Ryan doesn't respond.

"There's a rope—there," Hana says, pointing. Heathcliff is naturally already headed for it. The rope is tied to a rock on either end, and stretches across the fast-moving water.

"What? We're supposed to use a tightrope to get across?" Ryan asks, skeptical.

"It doesn't look too tight," Blade points out. It's true. The rope isn't very taut. We couldn't walk on it even if we wanted to. Heathcliff wades into the water and grabs the rope. It becomes clear to us all instantly that we're supposed to walk across the raging rapids holding on to the rope.

"No way is that even possible," Ryan says, shaking his head. "We're not strong enough to pull ourselves against that water."

"Speak for yourself," Heathcliff says, grabbing on. He slips off his backpack and uses it as a kind of harness, strapping himself to the rope with it. Then he offers his hand to me to help me with mine. I climb onto a rock and turn as Heathcliff straps me in.

"That's crazy—no way," Samir says, shaking his head. "Besides, did I mention I can't swim and that I'm totally scared of water?"

"No, but we just assumed you were," Blade says, giving Samir a playful smile. "Come on, it won't be that bad. And you don't have to swim, there's a rope."

"No way am I going in there," Parker says, shaking her head. "You guys can go on without me."

"Maybe I'll stay with Parker. You know, for her protection," Samir offers. Even Parker gives him a dubious look.

Before she can reply, the wind brings us the sounds of dogs barking.

"Did I say 'stay'? I meant I am totally going. Drowning is a great alternative to becoming kibble," he adds, scrambling into the water after us.

Heathcliff is first into the water and I slip my feet in after. It's freezing cold and sends a shock through my body even as my Converse get soaked.

"Oh my God, that's cold!" Samir shouts behind me. "Why didn't someone tell me about the cold?"

Parker and Ryan hesitate a few more seconds on the shore. But when it becomes clear the dogs are getting closer, even they wade into the water.

I walk a few steps, pulling on the rope as I go, sticking close to Heathcliff. So far, the water doesn't seem so deep here, and it laps just above my ankles. The rocks are slippery, but so far I've managed not to fall.

"Maybe this isn't going to be so bad," I say.

Heathcliff glances back at me, a crooked smile on his face. This makes me think I've spoken too soon. The barking is getting louder. Heathcliff moves a little faster and so do I.

Behind us, I hear Parker mumbling her complaints, and a quick glance back and I see that Ryan isn't very happy, either. Samir is looking at the water with trepidation.

"We're halfway there," I shout back, trying to give them some encouragement. And it's true, we are. Twenty more feet and we're home free.

That's when ahead of me the water abruptly rises almost up to Heathcliff's waist. I wonder if he's fallen, but it occurs to me that he hasn't. The water has just gotten suddenly and decidedly deeper. I stop, but Blade is right behind me, and she bumps into me and sends me over into the deep.

"Aaaah!" I shout, as I plunge into the water next, the ground suddenly giving way, and the water rising to my chest. Heathcliff is much taller than I am. The water is freezing, and it's a lot harder to walk in the strong current when most of your body is under water.

"Whoa, sorry," Blade says, jumping in after me. Hana follows her, but Samir stops in his tracks.

"Oh no, no way," Samir says, shaking his head. "I'm not going in like that."

A dog appears on the shore where we came from, snarling and snapping its jaws. A second and third join him, and they sniff at the water and bark at us. None of them follow us in, though.

"We can't stop now," Ryan says. He's the last in the line and just ten or so feet from the dogs.

"Yeah, move it!" Parker shouts. "What's the holdup?" Parker's in a frenzy now that the dogs are close, and one or two of them seem to be contemplating jumping into the water after us. She gives Samir a hard shove and he falls forward, losing his footing. Suddenly, he's swept up by the current and is on the surface of the water, struggling to get control. The only thing keeping him from being swept downriver is his backpack, which is still hooked securely to the rope.

"If you don't move, I'm going to have to make you go," Parker says, and starts fiddling with Samir's backpack.

It's evident to all of us at once that Parker plans to cut Samir free. And since he can't swim, he'll most certainly drown.

"Parker! What are you doing?" says a desperate Samir, even as Parker manages to unhook Samir's backpack. Now he's simply holding on to the rope without a safety line. "Parker! Please!"

"Parker! Stop it!" Hana shouts as she tries to intervene.

"Leave him alone," Blade seconds, throwing her hands into the mix.

But Parker is determined, and as we watch, she starts to pry Samir's fingers off the rope.

"Look out! One of them is coming in!" Ryan shouts, drawing my attention away from Samir, and I turn to the beach just in time to see that one of the dogs has taken a few steps back from shore. Then he hunches down, his muscles tense and ready to leap. And just as suddenly, the dog springs into the water and heads straight for Ryan.

Fifteen

"Come on!" I shout to Samir. "We've got to move!"

"We are!" Blade says, and she and Hana working together somehow manage to get Samir on his feet again, no thanks to Parker, who was two fingers away from sending him to a watery grave.

Once Samir is moving again, Parker and Ryan leap forward into the deeper part of the river, just in time. The dog quickly finds itself in deeper water with a stronger current. It starts paddling, but the water is too swift, and he's quickly flung downstream.

Seconds later, Heathcliff lands on the opposite shore and pulls me out. The rest follow us, and we all stand, panting and dripping wet, watching the two remaining dogs bark and howl on the other side of the river. Neither of them will follow us, I'm pretty sure.

Samir's teeth are chattering, in part from the cold,

and partly because he nearly drowned, and I throw my arm around him and give him a hug to try to help warm him up.

Parker shrugs off her jacket nonchalantly and wrings the water out of it.

"My shoes are ruined thanks to you," Parker says, glaring at me. I can't believe my ears. She nearly killed one of our friends and all she cares about is her shoes.

"Your *shoes*! Who gives a shit about your shoes?" Blade shouts, angrier than I've ever seen her.

"They're Burberry, and worth more than *your life*," Parker hisses.

Blade, who is fuming, steps right into Parker's face.

"You nearly killed him," she grinds out, pointing to Samir, who's still a little pale from the experience. "You *knew* he can't swim. What was he going to do if you pulled him off that rope?"

"It's not my problem," Parker snaps.

"Well, I'm about to *make* it your problem," Blade says, and shoves Parker hard in the chest, sending her flying backward into the mud. Parker scrambles up, murder in her eyes, and charges for Blade, who is braced for impact and a good fight. All of us stare, slack-jawed, except for Ryan, who steps quickly into Parker's path.

"That's enough," he says, catching her before she

makes contact with Blade. "We don't have time for this."

"Oh, I have time, believe me," Blade says, still furious.

"We're losing daylight, and we need to find Lindsay," Ryan says. "Save the grudges for when we're back on campus, okay?"

Blade glances at me, and then back at Parker. "Fine," she says, but she doesn't like it.

"Whatever." Parker shrugs.

"Now," Heathcliff says, "we head east."

He turns and leads us in the right direction, taking us deeper into the forest than I've ever been. The forest is thick and overgrown, and the farther we walk, the denser the trees and brush seem to get. At one point, I can't even really see much of the sky through the tall branches above our heads. My wet clothes hang heavily on my back, as we walk for what seems like forever. I don't know how long we trudge through the forest, but after a while, even my clothes are mostly dry. My shoes, however, are a different story. I feel something gross and squishy between my toes, and I don't know if it's my sopping wet socks or mud or what.

Blade is in front of me now and Parker's behind. Hana and Samir and I are in between them to prevent any more fights, although I wouldn't have minded seeing Blade teach Parker a lesson. Parker, for her part, will not shut up. She's tired, or her feet hurt, or she doesn't think we're going in the right direction. Or she's thirsty. Or hungry. Or cold. I'm so annoyed by Parker's running commentary that I don't even notice when we hit a particularly muddy patch. My right foot sinks into a foot of sludge.

I tug hard to get it out, but Heathcliff is there with strong hands to lift me straight out of the mire and onto relatively drier ground.

"Careful," he says. For a second, I'm sucked into his dark eyes. "Here, let me take this," he adds, grabbing my backpack and putting it over his shoulder. My back feels so much better freed of the weight. I smile at him in relief. He returns the smile, and I'm amazed how much different his face looks when he smiles. He's not quite so dark and brooding, even though he still looks a little bit dangerous. Heathcliff always manages to look dangerous.

"You sure you want to do this?" Heathcliff asks me, eyes now serious. "You know, I could find her for you. You know I'd do that for you."

I look at him and I know it's true. At that moment, I'm pretty sure he'd do almost anything I asked of him. That knowledge gives me a little rush.

"I know, but this is something I have to do," I say. "She's my sister."

Heathcliff nods.

The moment between us is broken by the sound of Parker's voice somewhere behind me.

"This is, like, totally gross," she whines.

"What? Can't quite walk in those expensive shoes of yours?" Hana asks her.

"Shut up," Parker spits. "Agggh. Ryan! Help!" Parker loses both flats in the mud. Ryan slumps his shoulders and turns back to help Parker. Heathcliff, for his part, doesn't even slow down.

"Maybe you ought to consider Doc Martens," Blade says as she walks easily past the stuck Parker, clomping through the mud in her lace-up, thick-soled boots. On her way by, she gives Parker a little nudge and sends her buttfirst into the mud. She lands with a squishy sound and nearly sputters with rage. Ryan, however, keeps her from charging Blade and manages to calm her down enough not to fight. I have to hide a smile, though. Parker's little plaid mini is covered in gray sludge, as are her white leggings. I've never seen her look so bad, and I have to admit that I'm enjoying every minute.

"Do you notice something weird about this place?" Hana whispers in my ear as we trudge through the undergrowth.

"You mean aside from the fact that Samir is holding on to my backpack like we're on a kindergarten field trip?" Blade asks.

"I don't want to get lost, okay?" Samir says, letting go of Blade's strap.

"I mean, have you guys seen a squirrel? Or a chipmunk? Or a bird?" Hana asks us. I realize she's right. I haven't seen a single animal since we left campus, except for the attack dogs. No birds. No squirrels. Nothing. The only sounds in the forest are the wind in the trees and our footsteps.

A cold wind blows and I shudder suddenly. The creepy mood is broken by the whiney voice of Parker.

"This is disgusting!" Parker shouts, somewhere behind us. "This mud is never going to come out."

"Looks like homicidal homecoming queens are the only animal species making any noise around here," Blade says.

"Don't you think it's weird? I mean, there should be chipmunks or something," Hana says. "I've never been in woods that are this quiet."

"Hey, look, there's a bird, I think," Samir says, pointing toward a small break in the brush, where I can see a slash of blue. Maybe it is a bird. He pushes through, then jumps ahead of both me and Heathcliff. "Yeah, I think it is . . ."

He pushes through the brush toward the bright blue feathers, but then freezes in his tracks.

"Aggggh!" Samir backs away from his find. "Not a

bird. NOT a bird!" he stutters, backing straight into Heathcliff and stumbling over his feet.

I move closer to see what he's looking at, and see a bright headdress of blue and yellow feathers. Peering out from beneath it are the two empty eye sockets of a human skull.

Sixteen

The skull has been bleached white by the sun and is sitting on top of a pole with the elaborate, Indian-like headdress placed on its head. And it's not alone. There are two others, with smaller head-dresses, posted nearby. They seem to be guarding a small clearing.

"An Indian burial ground," Blade says, excitement in her voice as she pushes her way past us, walking straight by the skulls. My Goth friend is totally unfazed by skulls. Last year, she used to have a skull candle on her desk. "This is *so* cool," she exclaims, like a seven-year-old on Christmas morning. "We could *totally* be cursed right now."

"Only you would think Indian curses are cool," Hana says.

"Indian burial ground? Are you serious?" Samir asks, suddenly more anxious than usual. "Okay, nothing good ever happens on Indian burial grounds. *Poltergeist*? *Pet Sematary*? Anybody?"

I follow Blade into the clearing with Heathcliff not far behind me.

"Talk about anorexic," I hear Parker say behind us as she and Ryan see the skulls for the first time.

"Okay, guys? Why are you walking *on* the Indian burial ground?" Samir asks us as we explore. "Why aren't we running away? Am I the only one who ever watches horror movies? Seriously."

"Whoa, check this out!" Blade says, walking up to a kind of shrine, which looks a little like a totem poll, except it's made mostly of skulls.

"Do you know what it means?" Hana asks Blade.

"It means we should get the heck out of here, that's what it means," Samir says.

"What are you, *scared*?" Parker sniffs. She walks straight up to the totem shrine and just plucks a skull right off the top of the stack. "Of this?"

It figures that Parker would show no squeamishness when it comes to human bones. Given the rumors about why she got sent to Bard, it's no wonder that she's fine with having a Hamlet moment, with a skull in one hand and the other on her hip. She looks like she's about to deliver a soliloquy.

"Put that down," Blade tells Parker.

"Who's going to make me?" she asks. "You?"

"It's got to be bad luck," Samir points out.

"I don't believe in luck," Parker says, tossing the skull carelessly to the ground. Upon impact, the jaw breaks off. Blade sends her a death stare, but Parker's already moved on.

"Vandalizing an Indian burial ground, nice move," Samir says.

"Guys, this burial ground has been here a long while," Hana says. "It's more than five hundred years old."

She points to a stone marker. It's engraved in Spanish.

"Can you translate?" I ask her.

"Yeah," she says, and reads aloud.

SACRED GROUND,
CONSECRATED THIS YEAR OF OUR LORD, 1414,
IN HONOR OF THE DEAD WHO WALK AMONG US.

"I thought Columbus didn't discover America until 1492," Samir says, scratching his head and staring at the marker.

"More importantly, what do they mean by the 'dead who walk among us'?" Ryan asks.

I glance at Hana, Blade, and Samir. We know what they mean. Of course, neither Ryan nor Parker know about our famous ghost teachers.

But 1414? That's a long time before any of the teachers got here, that I know anyway. Interesting. I glance at Hana and can tell she's thinking the same thing. Most of the ghosts on campus arrived there in the nineteenth century or later, with a few exceptions. But none of them died in the 1400s.

"It's probably fake," Parker says, kicking the stone with one toe of her muddy shoe. The girl has no respect for anything, except Prada.

"It's real enough," Heathcliff says, speaking for the first time. "This island holds a lot of secrets."

"What's that supposed to mean?" Parker asks, but Heathcliff doesn't answer. He just falls silent as he stares at the ground.

"Footprints," he says. "Fresh ones."

I look where he's looking and see tracks in the shape of my Steve Madden loafers, the ones that Lindsay stole from me. At least, they've got the same heart-shaped sole and the Steve Madden logo on the heel.

"Those are Lindsay's!" I say. "She's been all over here."

"And she's not the only one," Hana says, pointing to another set of tracks. These are bigger, and some of them look like bare feet.

Heathcliff kneels down to study them.

"There was a struggle," he says, pointing to scuff marks in the mud. "I think these men took Lindsay."

I look down and it seems like Heathcliff is right. Lindsay's prints disappear right at the edge of the burial ground. And then it's just the larger footprints from then on.

"Maybe the ghost Indians got her," Samir says. We all stare at him as if he's insane. "What? Am I the only one with cable TV? I mean, seriously."

"Ghosts don't leave footprints, Samir," Blade says, as if pointing out the obvious.

"That's not true. Ms. W does," Samir says.

"What did you say?" Ryan asks Samir.

"What are you talking about?" Parker chimes in.

Samir quickly backtracks. "Um, nothing. I mean, bad joke."

"Since when do you ever tell a *good* joke?" Blade pokes Samir in the ribs.

"What happened to my sister? Can you tell?" I turn to Heathcliff. I have a sudden flash of Lindsay being bound and gagged like the student we saw in the woods being carried off by the pirates, or whatever it was we saw last night. A cold chill slinks down my spine. I hope nothing bad has happened to her.

"They got her here," Heathcliff says, pointing to the mud. "And I think they carried her off in that direction."

"You think it was the people we saw before?" I ask him. He nods.

"You're saying she was kidnapped? That's absurd," Parker says, appearing between Heathcliff and me. "Who would take a Bard student? Especially out here. This island is deserted."

"No it isn't," I say. "We saw a gang take a Bard student just last night."

"Even better, they were pirates," Blade adds.

"Pirates?" Parker echoes, suddenly becoming serious. Instead of scoffing, she seems to actually believe us.

"What do you know?" I ask her, thinking that maybe she's seen them, too.

"Nothing," Parker shrugs. "Rumors. Ghost stories."

"What stories?" I demand. But before Parker can answer, I hear a steady rumble in the distance. At first I think it might be thunder, but it's got a rhythmic quality, too steady to be thunder.

"Guys? Do you hear that?" Samir asks quietly.

"Hear what?" Parker snaps, but even as the words leave her mouth, her mouth goes slack. She hears it, too.

"Drums," Hana whispers.

"Awesome," Blade breathes. "Do you think they're cannibals?"

"Shut *up*," Parker hisses, but I can tell she's scared. Just like the rest of us. It's hard to keep your composure with the strong, steady beat of drums in the distance. It doesn't help that the sun is setting. It'll be dark soon.

"It's getting dark," Samir points out, as if we all hadn't noticed the dwindling daylight.

"Looks like your little detour took longer than it should've," Ryan says. "If we'd headed east, we would've been there by now."

Heathcliff frowns at Ryan. "We would've been eaten alive by the dogs first," he says. "Or worse."

"What's the worse?" Samir asks, but seeing the scowl on Heathcliff's face, backtracks. "Um, never mind. Forget I asked."

"Ryan, let's go back," Parker says. "We can't afford to break curfew."

Ryan looks at me and then back at Parker. He seems conflicted.

"But we promised we'd help," Ryan says.

"Help, not kill ourselves trying." Parker hugs her arms around herself as if suddenly very cold.

"How much farther, Heathcliff? Can we make it before dark?" I ask.

Heathcliff looks down at the mud and then up at me. He shakes his head. "We'd be better off camping here for the night and waiting until daylight."

"This is insane," Ryan says.

"Agreed," Samir says. "Camping near an Indian burial ground? Doesn't anyone else think that's a bad idea?"

"Not to mention the kidnappers are on the loose," Hana points out. The sun seems to have set in record time and it's so dark that I can barely make out the expressions on the others' faces. There's a pause in conversation and we all listen to the steady beat of the drums in the distance. They go *thud, thud, thud.*

"I'm not camping anywhere," Parker says, her voice high and squeaky. She mentioned ghost stories. Do they have something to do with this? I need to find out what she knows.

"Parker, just tell me what you know. What stories did you hear?"

"Forget it," she says, brushing me off. "I'm going. I mean it."

She's scared. I don't blame her. The drums are pretty unnerving. She looks over at Ryan. When he doesn't immediately jump to attention, Parker whirls around and starts off without him. "Fine if you stay, but I'm going."

"I wouldn't do that if I were you," Heathcliff says.

"Well, I don't really care what you think," Parker huffs, and then starts off back the way we came.

"Parker, wait!" Ryan exclaims, bounding after her.

"She's crazy to try to walk in the dark," Heathcliff tells me, as he clears off some nearby brush to make the fire. In the distance, the drums abruptly stop.

And then, through the darkness, in the direction Parker ran, comes a high-pitched scream.

Seventeen

Hana, Blade, and I take off toward the sound of the scream. Heathcliff and Samir lag behind. About fifty feet from the Indian graveyard, we find Ryan peering down into a large hole.

"Careful," he says, holding his hand up as we approach.

It's a trap—a big hole that was covered up with leaves and sticks—and down in the muddy depths below is Parker, who is curled up in a ball and holding her ankle.

"I'm going to sue you," she hisses at us as we lean over to take a look. "My dad will sue this whole damn school for everything it's worth."

"Parker, just try to stay calm," Ryan says. "We'll get you out somehow."

"She's lucky she didn't break her neck," Blade says, although she sounds a little disappointed.

Hana whips out a flashlight from her backpack and shines it down on Parker, who blinks back the light and shades her face from it. Ryan tries to reach a stick down to Parker, who lunges at it, but can't quite reach.

"Maybe if you hold my legs," Ryan asks us, looking from me to Blade and then to Hana.

"We need someone stronger," Hana points out.

"Like Heathcliff," Blade says. "Otherwise, you'll end up in the hole with Parker. Of course, if you want some time alone with Princess Psycho, then that's fine."

"I can hear you, you freak!" Parker shouts from the hole.

Ryan just frowns at Blade.

"I'll get Heathcliff," I say.

"We'll both go."

Heathcliff has managed to get a little fire started and he's gathering more wood to put into it.

"We need some help," Ryan says, but Heathcliff ignores him. "Parker is trapped."

Heathcliff barely pauses in his wood gathering.

"Are you just going to ignore us?" Ryan asks.

"I warned her," Heathcliff mutters.

Heathcliff doesn't even look at Ryan. He just pokes at the fire. I put my hand on his arm, and he looks up at me.

"I don't like her, either, but we can't leave her there," I say.

He blinks at me and then scowls. "You want me to help her?" he asks me, his eyes darker and more brooding than usual. He doesn't like Parker. Helping her would go against every instinct he has.

I nod.

Heathcliff sighs, but straightens, looking resigned. "Anything you ask of me, I'll do."

Back at the sinkhole, Heathcliff has Ryan hold his feet. Within a matter of minutes, he's pulled Parker out. Typical of Parker, she doesn't bother to thank him.

"Hey, watch it!" she cries as he tugs on her wrists. He glances up at me and I give him a warning look. I can tell he wants to drop her straight back down in the pit. I know how he feels.

As soon as Parker is on safe ground again, Ryan immediately starts to help her hobble back to the camp that Heathcliff has set up for us. There's now a small fire, which we huddle around because it's starting to get cold.

"So what do you think they'll do to us when we get back?" Samir asks.

"Dish duty?" Hana offers.

"*Pffft.* Only if we're lucky," Blade says. "Toilet duty is more likely. Or maybe figurative expulsion."

Everybody looks at me after she says this. It's because last semester I got this punishment when the faculty wrongly thought I'd caused the disappearance of two teachers. Figurative expulsion means that basically everybody ignores you, as if you don't exist.

"Being a social pariah is the worst by far," I say.

"Of course, you were one of those even before you got ex-communicated," Parker snaps. Her hurt ankle is making her even ruder than usual. "Anyway, I'm not getting anything because I didn't want to spend the night out here in the first place."

I have the distinct impression that the minute we get back to campus she's going to blame everything on me, even though she was the one who volunteered to tag along. Maybe she and Lindsay do have something in common, after all.

"No one's going to get in trouble," Ryan says. "All we do is say that we got lost, and then Parker hurt her ankle, and we couldn't go back before curfew. They can't punish us for trying to help Parker."

Parker sniffs, but doesn't say anything. She just cuddles up to Ryan for warmth. Ryan lets her. Fine, I think. If *that's* the way he's going to play it. First, he crushes on my sister, and then he lets Parker fawn all over him? Two can play that game.

I scoot closer to Heathcliff. He's momentarily surprised, given that public displays of affection are strictly verboten since the faculty forbade us to get together. After a second, Heathcliff rolls with it, though, and lays a hand softly on my back. Absently, he starts rubbing my neck. It feels good, too good.

I notice curious stares from Hana. She knows Heathcliff is off limits. Everyone does. But then again, there aren't any teachers here. And my neck hurts. Not to mention my pride. If I have to watch Parker throw herself at my ex, then the least I can do is show them both I've moved on.

Parker glances at Heathcliff and Ryan takes notice, too. He stiffens a little. Well, let him stew, I think. He's the one who volunteered for this little adventure.

"So, Heathcliff," Ryan says, "I don't think I know where you're from."

Heathcliff looks up sharply and glares at Ryan. He has no interest in talking to Ryan, now or ever. He stares, mute.

"Somebody said 'Wuthering Heights,' " Parker says, snickering a little. "But everyone knows that's not a real place."

Heathcliff's body tenses. He doesn't like being laughed at. Especially by people like Parker. I can feel the anger in him welling. I put a hand on his arm to try to calm him down. I send Parker a warning look, but she ignores it. I cover Heathcliff's hand with my own, willing him to be calm.

"Come on, Miranda, what do *you* say?" Parker says.

"Looks like you know Heathcliff pretty well. Just where does he come from?"

"England," I say. This isn't a lie.

"*Everybody* knows that—his accent, duh," Parker says, kicking out one foot to underline her point, but she actually makes contact with a twig in the fire and sends it flipping in my direction. The flame lands on my blanket and sparks fly. Everything happens so quickly, I don't even have time to react. Heathcliff is there, though, quick as a flash, using his jacket to suffocate the fire before it even starts. I look up and notice that Parker is grinning. Even if it wasn't on purpose, she's still enjoying the fact that she nearly burned me alive.

"Apologize," Heathcliff growls at Parker now. He's got his fist clenched at his sides. He means business, and he doesn't care if Parker is a girl or not, he might just use force. Across the fire, Blade smirks. She's enjoying this.

"I didn't mean to," Parker says.

"That's not an apology." Heathcliff's voice is like steel. It's times like these that I remember reading about his temper in *Wuthering Heights.* Parker had better do what he says.

Parker pales a little, but she's stubborn and she doesn't want to give in.

"She wasn't even hurt," Parker says, her voice weaker, though.

Heathcliff makes a move toward her and she flinches.

"Hey, dude, it was an accident," Ryan says, standing, too. What is he *doing*? Getting in Heathcliff's face is a suicide mission and why is he defending Parker? She did almost light me on fire. And accident or not, she enjoyed it.

"You know a lot about accidents," Heathcliff says, the flames from the fire casting dancing shadows on his face. I look at him sharply. Does he know about Ryan's car accident?

"What is that supposed to mean?" Ryan asks, suddenly defensive.

"You know what it means," Heathcliff says. So he does know. Interesting. Where did he hear that? I never told him. "Maybe you should spend less time trying to protect girls like Parker and more time thinking about what you did."

"Do you have a problem with me?" Ryan sputters, his face flushed and angry, as he steps in closer, nose to nose with Heathcliff. I suspect this is going to get very ugly very quickly. Ryan is built like a basketball player; Heathcliff like a linebacker. If the two of them actually got into a fight, Heathcliff would win hands down, and Heathcliff knows it, too. Ryan, however, seems to be oblivious to this fact.

"What? Is someone a little too sensitive?" Heathcliff smiles, slowly and methodically, deliberately baiting Ryan, and Ryan rises to the bait. He whirls and punches Heathcliff in the mouth, taking Heathcliff by surprise. It's an awkward punch, though, and doesn't even cause Heathcliff to take a step backward. Heathcliff rubs his jaw, at first looking surprised, as if he can't believe Ryan touched him. Then, angry, his eyes go cold. Ryan should get out of the way, but he doesn't, he braces for impact. Heathcliff is also faster than he looks. Ryan probably couldn't have ducked even if he wanted to. Heathcliff's fist smashes into Ryan's jaw, and Ryan wheels backward, flying almost like a boxer in a cartoon, straight off his feet, landing flat on his back, blood springing from his lip and nose. Heathcliff hit him so hard, he's momentarily dazed, lying completely still.

"You killed him!" screams Parker.

Heathcliff isn't finished then, even, and marches toward Ryan as if he actually plans to finish the job. Before I know what I'm doing, I step in between, shielding Ryan with my own body.

"That's enough," I say, believing that however mad he is, Heathcliff won't hurt me. I'm right, because he stops in his tracks. His face deepens into a bitter scowl.

"You choose him over me?"

Before I have a chance to answer, Parker pipes in.

"You might as well give up now, Heathcliff." Parker smirks. "It's clear she doesn't want you."

Heathcliff's face turns deep red and then white, his lips set in a thin line. Without saying a word, he just turns and stomps off into the woods, whipping branches away from his face.

"Shut up, Parker," Blade says, but I don't wait to see if she does. I head after Heathcliff. He's walking so quickly that I only manage to catch up with him after about twenty paces.

"Heathcliff! Wait! Heathcliff . . ." I call after him. I finally get close enough to touch his shoulder, and that's when he whirls on me, his face a mask of anger and hurt. He grabs my wrist and suddenly thrusts me against a tree, his eyes dark and angry. I have a flash of sudden worry. Is he going to hit me?

Was Ms. W right? Is Heathcliff simply bad to the core? I suddenly think I might be playing with fire, thinking that I can control him, when he's not controllable. My hands are over my head, held there tightly by Heathcliff, and I'm helpless.

I must look a little scared, because he releases his grip on my wrists. Our faces are close now.

"You must know that we belong together," he tells me. Then suddenly he's kissing me, hard and fierce, his lips covering mine, nearly suffocating me. Just as quickly as it began, it ends as he pulls away. This time, I'm too stunned to follow after him as he thrashes his way through the woods.

Eighteen

A little dazed, I walk back to camp. When I get there, I find them all talking about Heathcliff.

"That guy is a menace," Parker is telling Ryan. She's hovering over him, naturally, trying to take care of him. Parker as the Nurse Nightingale type, though, is a little far-fetched. I can't imagine she actually has a maternal instinct. It's got to all be for show. Ryan, for his part, is waving off her attentions. He catches my eye.

"You still think you can trust him?" he asks me, a challenge.

"We don't have a choice," I tell him, sidestepping his question. Part of me does trust Heathcliff, unconditionally. But another part is worried that his temper is something that even he can't control. Still, Ryan has been in his face. It's no wonder he snapped. Not to mention, it was Ryan who hit Heathcliff first, I remind myself.

"We should go back to campus *now,*" Parker whispers.

"I don't know," Hana says.

"We can't go," I say, ducking beneath a low-lying branch and plopping down beside Hana. "Heathcliff knows the best route. Without him we'd be lost."

Ryan snorts. "Which is why he's taking us everywhere on this island *except* Whale Cove."

"We had to avoid the dogs, remember?"

"I don't know why you stick up for him," Parker says. "He's a bully. Maybe he's even responsible for Lindsay."

"We both know who's responsible for Lindsay coming out here," I grind out. "And it's *not* Heathcliff."

"You still on that trip?" Parker scoffs. "I thought you'd eventually get rid of your paranoid delusions."

"They're not—" I start, but Hana interrupts me.

"Maybe Parker is right," Hana says. "I mean, we don't actually know if we can trust Heathcliff."

"Not you, too," I say, feeling a little betrayed. "Heathcliff has saved us more than once."

"Saved you? How?" Ryan asks. His eyes flash in the firelight. Is he jealous?

"He also kidnapped us," Samir reminds me. That was back during my first semester at Bard, when Heathcliff was working for Emily Brontë. The same Brontë of *Wuthering Heights* fame, the one who tried to destroy the school because she couldn't stand another day of purgatory. Back then, Heathcliff had been under her influence, and a pretty powerful influence it was. She was his creator, after all. Now, he was free to make his own decisions.

"Kidnapped?" Ryan echoes, lips settling into a thin line. "See? You can't trust him. I knew it."

"Guys, it doesn't matter," Blade points out. "It's too dark to find our way out now anyway, even if we did want to leave without him."

This is true. It's pitch-black, and somewhere out in the distance there are more drum beats. I shiver. I suddenly wish Heathcliff would come back. Absently, I touch my chin where his stubble rubbed it a little raw.

"Samir is right," Hana says.

Everyone seems to agree on this. The idea of heading into the woods in total darkness doesn't appeal to anyone. The safest place seems by the fire Heathcliff built.

We sit in silence, each of us staring into the fire.

Now's my chance to try to figure out what Parker knows about pirates. Maybe she heard or saw something that could help us. I decide to swallow my anger and try to ask her again.

"Parker," I say, catching her eye, "you said you heard rumors about pirates. What did you mean?"

Parker shrugs. "It's just a ghost story I heard," she says.

"Ghost story?" Samir asks, his voice wavering a little. Samir is no fan of ghost stories.

"What? You afraid?"

"No," Samir lies. "I've just heard them all. Are you going to tell me about the hook in the car door? Or saying Bloody Mary's name in front of a mirror? Or—no, wait—the people who steal your kidneys and leave a note that says 'go to a hospital—you're missing a kidney'?"

"No. This one is about a pirate ghost, on this very island."

"Pirates aren't scary," Blade says, unimpressed.

I think back to the ones I saw in the forest. The ones that kidnapped the Bard student. Pirates definitely can be scary.

"Lindsay was the one who heard the story, she said a teacher told it to her," Parker says.

My ears perk up. Teacher? Hana catches my eye. She knows this is important, too. If a teacher had been telling Lindsay a story, then it's probably true. And if it's a teacher like William Blake, then he's been manipulating Lindsay to get what he wants. Blake went a little crazy last semester and tried to bring about the apocalypse. Blake hears voices, and not all of them are friendly.

"Who?" I ask.

Parker shrugs. "I don't remember."

"Think, Parker. Who did she say it was?"

"I don't *know*, God, and anyway, who cares?" Parker rolls her eyes. She doesn't know why this is a big deal. Of course, she has no idea said teachers are ghosts in the first place. Or how what Lindsay said could be a bigger clue in her disappearance. For the first time, I wonder if maybe Parker wasn't behind Lindsay's escape into the forest. Did a teacher put her up to it? I feel a cold hardness in my stomach. If so, then this is even worse than I thought. Hana and I exchange glances. I can tell she's thinking the same thing.

"Do you want to hear the story or not?" Parker asks, still peeved.

"No," Samir says.

"Yes," Hana, Blade, and I all say at once.

"Fine, story it is," Parker says, clapping her hands together. "Okay, so, like, two hundred years ago or whatever, this island was a place where a pirate named Peg Leg hid his ship and his treasure. Now, Peg Leg was a particularly nasty pirate. He lost his leg in a gunfight and was still pretty ticked off about it. So whenever he would catch prisoners on his ship, he'd cut off their legs with his rusty saw to get them to talk."

"Rusty saw?" Samir asks. "So they'd get their legs cut off *and* get tetanus? That's just cold, man."

Parker glares at Samir, but continues her story.

"He'd throw the legs overboard and, with all the

blood and everything, sharks would come to eat them."
Parker's eyes gleam in the firelight. She seems to be really relishing the gross bits of this story. Why I find this surprising, I don't know. It's Parker, after all. "And when the sharks came, Peg Leg would throw his prisoners overboard, too, so that they would be devoured. Alive."

"Is this a pirate or a James Bond villain?" Samir asks.

Blade half laughs, half snorts. Parker ignores them both.

"Peg Leg carried a rusty old saw with him wherever he went. He used this rusty saw to cut off prisoners' legs. It was said he even slept with it by his side, and if anyone tried to take it, he'd cut off their fingers."

"Gross," Hana says.

"But Peg Leg was eventually captured by the British Royal Navy, and they hung him and most of his crew for piracy."

"I'm guessing that's not the end of Peg Leg," I say.

"Well, the odd thing is that they never found his rusty saw. Some say he buried it. Some say he hid it, but they never found it. Rumor has it that he and his crew haunt this very island," Parker says. "And that every full moon, they go out looking for prisoners. Peg Leg's ghost and his famous saw were reunited, and he uses it to this day."

I can't help but wonder if this legend and the pirates I saw last night are connected. Could it be that they're part of a ghost story? I wonder. Still, I don't remember any of them having a peg leg. Or a saw. But they were taking prisoners—the Bard student. I swallow, hard. Does that mean they plan to slice and dice him with a rusty old saw? I shiver and hug myself, hard. I really, really wish Heathcliff were here. Ryan looks at me across the fire. I can't tell what he's thinking. And I've got too much on my mind to worry about figuring it out.

"At least it's not a full moon," Samir interjects. He's looking up into the sky, which is covered by clouds. I can't see the moon at all. But then, as if on cue, the clouds above our heads part, revealing most of the top of a full moon.

"You were saying?" Hana says.

"Whatever, ghost stories are all about the full moons," Blade says. "But this one sounds far-fetched even for me to believe. I mean, ghost pirates? Is this an eighties flashback to *The Goonies* or what?"

I glance at Blade. Of course she's not scared. Very little scares her. Besides, she didn't see the pirates firsthand, like I did.

"I knew someone who saw Peg Leg," Parker insists. "Two years ago, I knew this guy who went out into the woods with his girlfriend, you know, to make out.

It was a full moon that night, and the two were getting it on, thinking no one was around. But then they heard the footsteps."

Pirates were here two years ago? I shudder.

"So the girl gets spooked and she insists on going back. But the guy doesn't want to leave. And then the girl screams, because she thinks someone was trying to take her backpack, and they both start running to campus, right? When they get there, the guy is really p.o.'d because he didn't get any, and that's when the girlfriend looks at him and screams."

Parker takes a dramatic pause, the light from the campfire making her face look distorted and slightly ghoulish.

"Because, hanging from his backpack," Parker says, serious, her eyes sharp as she looks at each one of us in turn, "was a rusty saw."

Nineteen

We're all silent for a long moment, and then Blade breaks the tension by bursting out laughing.

"You call *that* a ghost story?" Blade wheezes. "Please!"

"Um, yeah, that was lame," Hana adds.

"Oh, totally lame," Samir chirps, even though he looks a little unnerved. Glad I'm not the only one. "Total hook-in-the-car-door ripoff."

"Now, I could tell you a *serious* ghost story," Blade adds.

"No!" Samir and Hana and I say at once.

"I think we've had enough ghost stories for one night," I add.

"Fine, suit your weenie selves," Blade sniffs, and then settles under her blanket. Within minutes, she's snoring. Nothing scares that girl. Or keeps her from a good night's sleep.

"She can sleep through anything," I tell Hana. Which, unfortunately, is not the case for me.

Between Parker's ghost story and the fact that Heathcliff hasn't come back, I'm not much in the mood for sleep. I lay awake for what feels like hours. Before I came to Bard, ghost stories never scared me. Of course, now that I'm here, I know that ghosts are very, very real.

After lying in the cold for hours, I somehow drift off to sleep, only to wake again with the distinct impression something is wrong. I sit up and blink back sleep, only to find that the fire has gone out. It's still dark and I shiver, wrapping the blanket closer around my shoulders. Somewhere nearby an owl hoots, above my head the clouds part, and the full moon gleams above my head, casting a silvery light across everything.

I look around me and see that I'm alone at the burned-out campfire. No Heathcliff. No Ryan. No Parker. No Samir, Hana, or Blade.

What in the world . . . ?

And then I hear the sound of footsteps nearby in the woods, somewhere over in the dark where the Indian burial ground is, and the chill that's outside seeps inside my chest and I shiver. Could it be Heathcliff? Or Ryan? Or those strange men I saw in the woods? A branch snaps and I jump a little. I don't feel like waiting around by myself to figure out who it is. I slowly creep away from my blanket and head to the woods, where I take cover behind a large tree. I scan the cemetery, looking for any sign of movement, anything to explain the sound of footsteps. I think I see a shadow move here and there, but I can't quite make out if it's a person or not.

Another branch cracks, but this time the sound comes from behind me. I whip around, my eyes scanning the dark. I want to ask if someone's there, but my voice dries up in my throat and I'm not sure where to hide. Quickly, I duck into the bushes, holding my breath. My heart is thumping so hard against my chest I think it might pop out.

Okay, I tell myself, I'm going to feel so stupid when it turns out that this is Heathcliff or Ryan or Samir. I'm going to feel so . . .

My thoughts disappear, as through the bushes I see a boot step in front of me. It's black and well worn, but that's not what catches my eye. Instead of having a pair, the man's other leg is . . . a wooden peg.

Peg leg? Seriously? Parker's ghost story pirate?

I freeze. My pulse quickens and my heart thumps loudly in my chest. I'm praying Peg Leg just moves on. I'm pretty attached to both my legs, thanks. I don't want either one sawed off.

But then the unthinkable happens. Two strong arms dive into the bush and grab me and suddenly I'm struggling and screaming.

And then, inexplicably, I'm face-to-face with Ryan.

"You were having a nightmare," he says, and I realize he has both hands on my shoulders.

I look around. I'm lying down right where I fell asleep and the fire is still burning. I let out a long breath. Peg Leg was just a dream. A stupid Parker dream.

"Are you okay?" Ryan asks, looking concerned. "You were shouting."

"I'm fine," I say, feeling suddenly very embarrassed. It's bad enough to have my ex-boyfriend see me with bed head, but he's also now a witness to my crazy sleep rantings. Who knows what I said? Maybe I shouted out that I still loved him. But, of course, I don't actually. Do I? Looking at those perfect blue eyes, I'm not so sure anymore. "What did I say?"

"Nothing. You were just moaning and then shouting. Nothing I could understand," Ryan says. He still hasn't removed his hands from my shoulders. Ryan is staring at me a bit too intently. It's clear that he's got something else besides friendship on his mind.

"So Lindsay likes you?" I say, feeling suddenly uncomfortable as I try to steer his blue gaze away from me. "And I just want to say that it's okay with me, I mean, if you like her, too." Of course, I am totally lying. It's *not* okay if he likes her. Even if he is my ex.

A smile dances around the corners of his mouth.

He's amused by the idea, clearly. "Did Lindsay tell you that the only thing we talk about is you?"

"Me?" I don't have to act surprised. I am. Ryan leans forward and brushes a bit of hair out of my eyes. He looks at my hair, then my forehead, then my eyes, and finally settles on my lips.

"You know that I'm not even close to being over you," Ryan tells me softly. He puts his hand behind my head and draws me closer.

I'm full of conflicting emotions. Do I want to kiss him? Well, of course. Who wouldn't want to? His picture is practically under the entry for "gorgeous" in *Merriam-Webster's Collegiate Dictionary.*

But still, I can't help but think this seems to be moving a little fast—come to think of it, just like all my interactions with Ryan. They always move at light speed. And I always jump in with two feet only to find out he's holding something back from me. Like the fact that he never told me what happened with his ex, the one who died. That, even more than the virginity question, really came between us last semester. Because I pretty much gave up everything—even my own identity—to be his girlfriend. I went from being Miranda Tate to Ryan's Girlfriend pretty much overnight, and I don't know if I'm ready to jump back into a relationship where I'm the one who gives up everything and Ryan gets to hold back.

And, besides, I remember with a start, he's the one who told Parker I was a virgin.

"Wait—Ryan," I say, putting a hand on his chest. "Don't."

"What's wrong?"

"Have you been talking to Parker about us? Because she sure knows a lot." I can't bring myself to say "she knows I'm a virgin" out loud because it sounds so silly. My eyes dart over to where Parker is sleeping, although I don't see her. Maybe she's gone off to the woods to use the bathroom. I don't really care. I'm just relieved she isn't here to intrude.

Ryan looks down at his lap. "I'm sorry, Miranda. I didn't mean to tell her, but she's a good listener and I needed someone to talk to."

Parker? A good listener? What planet is Ryan on?

"Sorry, not good enough," I say, shaking my head. "If you want to tell her more things than you tell me, then maybe it's her you should be dating."

"Miranda, that's totally wrong," Ryan says, sighing and running his hand through his hair. "I don't tell her things I don't tell you."

"What about Rebecca? She said you talk about her all the time."

That name hangs in the air between us, heavy and hard.

Ryan looks like he's backed into a corner. "You really want to know about her? About what happened?"

"Of course I do."

Ryan sighs again. He knows there's no way out. "Fine." He pauses, then swallows. This is hard for him, I can tell.

"I'm listening," I say.

"I had been dating Rebecca for five months. She was, uh, my first."

"First girlfriend?"

"First everything," Ryan says.

This is a surprise. I didn't know Ryan lost his virginity to Rebecca. And that he's telling me this is really amazing. Usually guys never admit they had virginity to lose.

"But she wasn't a good girlfriend," Ryan continues. "She cheated on me. She drank a lot. She wasn't the perfect girl everyone thought she was."

Given that she was one of Parker's friends, it doesn't surprise me.

"That night, she had had way too much to drink, but she wanted to drive. I told her no, that I would drive, because I hadn't been drinking. This made her furious, but eventually I got her in the front seat. But then she started telling me that she had been sleeping with Connor, my best friend. She threw it in my face."

Ouch. "Oh, Ryan. I'm sorry."

"That's when I broke up with her, and then she

started to get physical. She started hitting me. Scratching at my face. I was afraid she was going to make us crash, so I shoved her."

I can't imagine Ryan raising his hand to anybody, but apparently he had, and to his own girlfriend. I'm not sure how I feel about that, but I shove the thoughts aside.

"She hit her head on the window and I thought I'd knocked her out. I was so freaked out by it, that I didn't see that the light up ahead had changed. I ran a red light and a car nearly hit us. When I swerved to miss it, that's when I hit the tree. And Rebecca, well, she never woke up."

I don't know what to say to this. It's horrible. I can't imagine what it would be like to experience something like that.

"I blame myself," Ryan says. "I should never have shoved her. I should've just pulled over and tried to reason with her. I let my temper get the best of me."

"It's not your fault," I say.

"But it is," Ryan says. "Because I was driving. And that's why I got sent to Bard. And that's also why I try to help Parker, because Parker was Rebecca's best friend and I feel like I owe her something. And if you don't want to have anything to do with me anymore, I'll understand. I killed her."

"What are you talking about? Ryan, this isn't your

fault. She was acting insane and her death was an accident."

"That's not what most people think."

"Well, I'm not most people," I say, smiling. He returns my smile.

"But there's something else. Something I didn't want to tell you."

"What?"

"It sounds stupid."

"Believe me, I bet it isn't. The stuff I've heard today . . . trust me, it can't be worse than that."

"I think my girlfriend, well, my whole life, was kind of like a book."

I get a sinking feeling in my stomach. His life was like a book? And that was before he even came to Bard. That was out in the real world, where fiction isn't *supposed* to come to life.

"What book?" I ask, my voice barely a squeak. There's a loud rushing sound in my ears. I realize it's blood pumping hard in my veins. Fear.

"Have you ever read *Rebecca*?" I shake my head. "Well," Ryan continues, "it's *just* like that book. I found it in Rebecca's backpack after the accident and, I dunno, I just started reading it and . . . it's so weird, but it really started to sound like her life and mine. But the even stranger thing is that Rebecca even *looked* like the girl on the cover of the book. They could be sisters or something, but it's probably all just a coincidence, right?"

I am literally speechless. It is probably, definitely *not* a coincidence. Ryan's Rebecca was the same Rebecca from the book, I'm more than certain of it. Somehow she'd become real. I'm suddenly taken by the knowledge that the powers of Bard extend far beyond Shipwreck Island. My mind is a whirl of questions. Does the faculty know about this? And what does this mean? When I go back home, will I have to face Dracula? Or William Blake's tiger?

My mouth is dry and my stomach flops. I realize that while I've made my peace with Bard, I also took solace in the fact that I could leave it, too, that there's a "real" world to go back to. One where crazy things don't happen. One where everything can be explained and there are no such things as ghosts or boogey men or fictional characters living and breathing. The idea that I don't have that refuge anymore makes me more than a little scared.

"Miranda? Are you okay? You look like you just saw a ghost," Ryan says, concerned.

I can't help it, I burst out with a nervous laugh. "Ghosts!" I exclaim, then snort another laugh again, thinking about the entire ghost faculty. "I see ghosts all the time!" And this suddenly makes me bubble up with nervous laughter that I can't seem to stop. It's official: I'm cracking up. Bard has finally driven me insane.

"Miranda, I know it's a silly story, but you have to believe that it just seemed so real," Ryan is saying now. Poor guy is trying to convince me *he's* the one who isn't crazy. I settle down now and get a hold of myself.

"No, no, it's not you," I say quickly. "I believe you. Really. I do. Honestly, more than you know."

Ryan looks a little relieved. "So you don't think I'm crazy?"

"No, I don't," I say. "In fact, I think there's something you need to know." I pause. I figure I have to tell him Bard's big secret. He has a right to know. He's been living it without even knowing it. I'm not supposed to tell, but Ms. W will have to forgive me once she realizes why I did it. Besides, he practically knows already. He just doesn't realize it.

"The stories from books do come to life," I tell him. "As do fictional characters. I used to think it was just here, on this island. You see, Bard isn't just a school. It's also a kind of purgatory. Our teachers aren't our teachers. They're really ghosts, dead authors who are stuck in limbo." I'm talking fast, realizing that I'm in a rush to tell him this secret. I've been bottling it up for a year and it's a relief to finally let him in on it. "I mean, they're famous ghosts. Like Coach H is really Ernest Hemingway.

And Ms. W is really Virginia Woolf. And Headmaster B is Charlotte Brontë."

Ryan is just looking at me, expressionless. I suddenly realize I'm not telling this right. It sounds so far-fetched. I backpedal.

"I mean, like, remember last year? The tiger that was loose on campus? That wasn't just a regular tiger. That tiger came from William Blake's poem. You see, it was fiction, but it came to life. And other fictional characters come to life, too." Ryan's face turns skeptical. My mind races, trying to think of another. "Heathcliff!" I exclaim suddenly, grabbing Ryan's arm with both hands. "You see, Heathcliff is really the Heathcliff from *Wuthering Heights*. That's why no one knows where he's from. Because he really is from a book."

Ryan frowns at the mention of Heathcliff's name.

"And even me," I say, rushing to tell him everything. "I'm part fiction. My great-great-great-grandmother or something was originally a character in *Wuthering Heights,* too. But she left the book, so she's not there anymore and . . . well, okay, that's too complicated, but anyway, I'm part fiction. So you see," I barrel on, ignoring the darkening look on his face, "Rebecca might have been the real Rebecca from the book. You aren't crazy at all," I finish, realizing that my entire explanation sounds super lame.

Ryan is silent for a moment, taking it all in. *Please*

believe me, I think. I'm telling the truth. One hundred percent. I give him a pleading look and squeeze his arm, but he shrugs away my touch.

He glances up at me, looking sad and more than a little hurt. "You don't have to make fun of me," he says at last.

"What? I'm not—"

"Seriously, Miranda. I open up and tell you something serious, and you just make a big joke out of it. Fine if you don't believe me, but don't make fun of me."

Ryan gets up and shakes off a few dried leaves from his pants.

"Ryan, I'm not making fun of you, I swear. I am totally serious." I try to grab at his hand, but he shakes it away. "I'm telling the truth!"

"Whatever," Ryan says, not meeting my eyes. "It was real funny. Ha-ha. I'm sorry I bothered you. Glad you got a good laugh out of it."

"I'm not laughing!"

Ryan turns his back on me just as Hana comes bounding out of the woods, looking a little out of breath.

"Parker's gone," Hana says, her face a knot of concern.

"What do you mean, 'gone'?" Ryan asks, turning toward Hana and ending our conversation. Dammit.

"I mean *gone*," Hana says, pointing to the place

where Parker had been sleeping, but there's still no sign of her. She hadn't come back in the time Ryan and I had been talking and, for the first time, I notice her blanket is gone and her backpack, too.

"Could she have gone to the bathroom?"

"That's what I thought, but she's been gone a while," Hana says. "I woke up because I thought I heard something. When I looked up, Parker was gone, so I tried calling her name, but she didn't respond."

Uh-oh. For some reason, I'm pretty sure this isn't just one of Parker's jokes.

"Maybe she went back to campus?" I ask, even though I know that's probably not likely.

"On that bad ankle?" Ryan interjects. "She could barely walk on it."

Hana and I stare at each other, neither one wanting to admit that maybe Parker's been taken—by the same people who took my sister.

"Do you think . . ."

"I don't know," I say, not willing to say it out loud. "Did you find footprints?"

"There were too many leaves on the ground. I couldn't really tell," she says.

"What's going on, guys?" asks a groggy Samir, waking up and rubbing his eyes.

"Yeah, what's with all the chattering?" Blade sighs,

stretching and throwing off her blanket. The sky above our heads is getting lighter, thankfully. Dawn is coming and not a minute too soon, either.

"Heathcliff hasn't come back and Parker is missing," I tell them.

"I *so* told her not to mess with that Indian burial ground," Samir says, crossing his arms. "You guys never listen to me, and see? I'm always right."

"So what are we supposed to do now?" Blade asks me.

"We should go back to campus," Ryan says, now not meeting my eyes. He's still very mad. "Maybe Parker went there."

"No," I say, shaking my head. "I'm not leaving my sister out here."

"Okay, am I really the only one who's ever seen a horror movie?" Samir asks. "When people start disappearing from the group, it generally means they've been hacked to pieces and it's time for all the people who *still have their limbs* to run as fast as they can!"

"You're such a wimp." Blade sniffs. "No one's been hacked to pieces . . . that we know of."

"It's still a likely possibility," Samir says. "And besides, Heathcliff was supposed to be our guide. We don't even know where we're supposed to go."

"We could find it ourselves," Ryan says, sounding confident. "We don't need Heathcliff. Lindsay said the cove was on the far side of the island, so all we have to do is head east."

"And just where is that?" Blade asks.

"Hang on," Ryan says, whipping out a compass from his pocket. It's a tiny one dangling from his keychain.

"How'd you get that past the Guardians at check-in?"

"Hid it inside my American civilization book," Ryan says, as if it's obvious. He stares at the compass, frowning at it. "Hmmmm. That's weird."

I lean over to look and see that the compass arrow is slowly spinning around counterclockwise. But it never seems to stop.

"Maybe it's broken," Ryan says, shaking it.

Hana and I look at each other.

"It's not broken," Blade says. "It's the island."

"You're telling me this island has an electromagnetic force field?" Ryan asks, his voice skeptical.

"I'm saying that a compass won't do you any good," Blade says. "Anyway, east is that way."

"How do you know?"

"Because the sun is rising that way," Blade says. "Besides, I know we're close."

"How?"

"Look up," she says.

I do and see seagulls circling above our heads.

"Okay," I say. "But we should leave a note for Heath-cliff in case he comes looking for us."

"And one for Parker," Ryan says.

Reluctantly, I agree.

Hana writes the notes, while I head back to the campfire to wrap up my blanket and get my backpack together. That's when I look down and see the foot-prints. They're inches from my blanket, from where I slept, and they're not normal footprints. There's one boot print and then a single round hole, as if someone with one leg was walking with a cane or a crutch.

A shiver goes down my spine.

"Um, is that what I think it is?" Samir asks, stand-ing next to me, his voice cracking a little bit as he looks down at the footprints.

I nod slowly.

"Peg Leg," I say.

Twenty

"It was probably just Parker trying to freak you out," Hana says, ever the voice of reason as she pushes her glasses higher up on her nose. Together we tromp through the forest in the direction we think is east.

"Of course, there is the little problem of Parker disappearing," Blade says. "Who does a practical joke and then disappears? Wouldn't she want to laugh at you?"

"Good point," I say.

"There's no such thing as Peg Leg," Ryan says, sounding dismissive. He glances at me, and then adds for good measure, "Just like there's no such thing as ghosts."

So he's still in denial. Fine, if he wants to be like that. I know the truth. If he wants to think I just made it up, then that's his prerogative. I'm done trying to convince him.

"Whatever," I shrug, not looking at him. If he wants to be mad, then I can be mad, too. He should've believed me. It shows he still doesn't really trust me, after all. I can't help but think that Heathcliff would believe me no matter what I said. If I told him the sky was orange, he'd believe it.

Of course, Ryan always has been skeptical of all things supernatural. It's what makes it so surprising that he even allowed himself to believe that the accident had anything to do with *Rebecca*. Most of the time he's just too practical and sometimes it's just plain annoying. You'd think he would've caught on by now that something isn't right with this place, but he's totally clueless.

"You guys believe what you want, but I still say we should've headed back," Samir says.

"You better stop your whining," Blade warns. "Don't you know the scared guy always gets killed first in horror movies?"

"Yes, and that's exactly why I want to go back. Don't you think I know I'm marked for death? I'm a minority *and* I'm a total wimp."

At that very moment, the drums start up again with their rhythmic *thump, thump, thump.*

"Is it just me or are they louder?" I ask Hana, who nods.

"We're moving closer to them," she adds, her voice a low whisper.

"What do you think they are?" I ask her.

"On this island? I'd expect anything. Cannibals, probably," Blade says. I can't help but notice that she sounds a little too hopeful.

"Does *anything* scare you?" Samir asks.

"Beauty pageants," Blade answers right away, flicking her black-and-red spiking hair away from her eyes with her fingers, which are covered in silver skull rings and topped with jet-black nails. "And the color pink."

The drums seem to be coming at first from our right, and then from our left. I'm beginning to think we're walking in circles.

"We should've waited for Heathcliff," I whisper to Hana, watching Ryan trudge ahead of us into the brush.

"Did you ever stop to think that maybe he wasn't coming back?" Hana asks me.

"He'd never just abandon us," I say sharply.

"Okay, but even if he didn't, what if he was taken by force? By whoever took Lindsay?"

I hadn't thought of that. Despite Heathcliff's bad-boyness, maybe he really is in trouble. We walk by a big oak tree that looks familiar—too familiar.

"I think we're walking in circles," I tell Ryan.

"We can't be," Ryan says. "I've been watching the sun."

"How can you even *see* the sun?" Blade asks him.

It's a fair question. The forest is so thick it's hard to see sunlight or shadows.

"We're not walking in circles," Ryan declares.

"Well, if we're not, then how come I've just found some of my footprints?" Blade asks, pointing downward in front of her. Her Doc Martens tracks are there, plain as day in the mud.

"That's impossible," Ryan sputters. "I know my way around the woods."

"Um, Blade?" Samir asks, his voice catching a little. "Are those your tracks, too?"

Samir is pointing down at the ground and just a little ways off from Blade's tracks are another set. A man's boot print and a single, round hole.

"Peg Leg is following us!" Blade exclaims.

"You sound like that's a good thing," Samir says.

"Well, no, obviously, but if he has something to do with Lindsay's disappearance, then maybe we're on the right track."

"There's no such thing as Peg Leg," Ryan says. "There has to be another explanation."

We fall silent. None of us really believes there's a practical, nonscary explanation.

I can tell we're all a little unnerved. Being lost in the woods is bad enough, but having a potentially ticked-off pirate/ghost who likes hacking off limbs following you around just makes matters worse.

As we continue on, Hana pulls me bac

"What if Peg Leg is Ahab?" she whispers.

"The captain from *Moby-Dick*?"

"Yeah. He lost his leg and uses a woode

get around. And since literary characters

getting loose, it makes sense."

I'm momentarily relieved until I remember that Ahab is completely insane and fixated on revenge.

"But what would he want with us? He was obsessed with finding a whale. And there aren't any whales around here."

"I don't know . . ."

"What are you guys whispering about?" Blade asks us, leaning in. Samir scurries closer, too, so that the four of us are scrunched together away from Ryan, who is trying to hack his way through the forest ahead of us.

"I think Peg Leg might be Ahab," Hana says.

"Who's Ahab?" Blade asks, a bit too loudly. Ryan stops and turns.

"I take it you didn't do your summer reading?" Samir asks.

Blade snorts. "As if *you* did," she says. I try to tell Samir to lower his voice because Ryan is coming into earshot, but he doesn't.

"No, obviously. But I did read Spark Notes," Samir says. "Ahab is the captain of the *Pequod,* the ship that after Moby Dick. And if he's Peg Leg, then we're totally safe because all he wants is a whale. I don't think any of us are whales."

"Not you guys, too," Ryan says, frowning. "Are you all in on Miranda's little joke, too?"

"Joke?" Samir asks. "What joke?"

"You guys think it's pretty funny just to laugh at me? Well, that's fine. Go ahead. I'm leaving."

Ryan's mouth settles in a thin line of determination and he turns on all of us and stomps ahead into the woods.

"What's his problem?" Blade asks.

"I tried to tell him the Bard secret," I admit.

Everyone whirls on me.

"You didn't!" Hana exclaims.

"That's classified, sister," Blade scolds.

"Totally top secret," Samir agrees.

"But why?" Hana asks.

I decide not to tell them all the particulars. Ryan probably wouldn't appreciate it. "He thought his life was mirroring a book and, well, I just told him that it could be, because of what Bard really is."

"Unbelievable," Blade says, shaking her head. "What? You've got to spill your guts anytime a remotely cute guy starts confiding in you?"

"Hey—I dated him for a whole semester and managed not to tell him that entire time."

"Oooh. Give the girl a medal!" Blade says, rolling her eyes.

"You can't just go around telling anybody we're going to school in purgatory," Samir says. "They'll think you're crazy."

I nod. This is very true.

"Not to mention what it does to the LITs," Blade adds. "We can't just go around admitting new members anytime you feel like spewing secrets."

"And what about the faculty? They're going to be pissed!" Samir lets out a low whistle.

Hana gives me a sympathetic look. "No they won't," Hana says. "It's clear Ryan doesn't believe Miranda anyway. So nobody has to worry about more LIT members, or what the faculty will think. Let's just drop it, okay, guys?"

Samir and Blade grumble a bit, but decide to let it go.

"So what do we do about Ryan?" I ask the group. "We can't just let him go off by himself."

Right about that time, just ahead of us there's a shout, then the sound of something big falling.

"Ryan!" I shout, and take off running. I break through the clearing, only to nearly fall straight off a cliff. I skid to a stop, balancing precariously on the edge of a precipice that must be at least a hundred-foot drop straight down. I flail my arms and just manage not to plunge headfirst. I regain my balance, just as Samir, Hana, and Blade join me.

"Watch out," I say, holding up my hands. The last thing I need is for them to collide into me and send me over the edge.

"Um, a little help?" comes Ryan's voice from somewhere below my feet. I drop to my hands and knees and peer over the edge. I see Ryan hanging by a root coming out of the side of the mud hill. He wasn't as lucky as I was.

"Hold on, we're coming," I say. I look at Samir.

"What are you looking at me for? I'm scared of heights," he says.

"And that's a surprise, why?" Blade says, but she's smiling.

"We need rope. Anyone got any?"

The three of them shake their heads. "We'll have to make some." I glance down at everyone's Bard Academy standard-issue backpacks. "Empty your bags. We can tie them together."

I hear scraping on the cliff wall. It sounds like Ryan is trying to climb up. I hear him slip, then curse as his body bangs hard against the cliff.

"Hang on, Ryan. We're going to throw you a rope, okay?"

Furiously, we work to tie our backpacks together. Once done, Hana, Blade, and Samir act as anchors, holding on to the backpacks as I lean over the edge of the cliff and lower the string of backpacks down.

"You call this rope?" Ryan asks, reaching up and trying to grab hold of the low-lying strap of the last backpack in the chain.

"Best we could do." I stretch a little lower, hoping to bridge the gap between the backpacks and Ryan. As I watch, Ryan lunges again for the strap, but misses, nearly losing his grip on the root.

"Hang on!" I shout, just as he manages to recover, grabbing the root in his right hand and steadying himself against the mud wall. I can see his feet aren't getting any traction, and little bits of dirt and rocks are falling to the ground below. It occurs to me that the wall could shift at any moment and we could find ourselves in the middle of a mudslide.

"Lower, guys!" I shout to Hana, Blade, and Samir, trying to get the backpacks closer to Ryan's reach.

"If we go much lower, we won't be able to hold on at all!" Blade shouts.

"That's as far as we can go," I tell Ryan, who tries again to reach the backpack strap. But this time, his foot slips on the mud and he loses his grip on the root. For a second, my heart goes into my throat as I see him slide straight down, arms flailing. Ryan manages to catch himself on another root just in time to stop his complete free fall. He's at least another two body lengths down the cliff and there's no way our back-packs can reach him now.

"Dammit," I hiss as Ryan curses and mutters to himself. "Maybe we can find something else to tie together!" I shout down to him, even though I know the outlook is bleak. There's no way for us to save him.

"No, forget it," Ryan says. "You'll just end up falling down here with me."

As I watch, Ryan looks for footholds. But instead of going up, he seems to be heading down.

"Where are you going?"

"I think it's easier just to go down," he says. "And besides, I think I see something down here. I think it might be the beach."

I look down, trying to see where he's looking, but there are still a few trees around the base of the cliff and it's hard to make out. The leaves and branches block our view. Ryan, however, is below the top of the trees and seems to be able to see what we can't.

"Yeah, there's the ocean," he says as he makes his way downward. "And wait. There's something more."

I lean down and watch him jump the last five feet down to the sandy ground. He shakes mud off his legs, then trots out of view for a second. He returns carrying a piece of paper. It looks like it's been ripped out of Lindsay's notebook.

"I think this is Lindsay's handwriting!" Ryan shouts, holding it up for me to see. He's right. "We're close."

"What does it say?" I shout down to him.

"Um . . ." He pauses, reading. "It looks like she's just practicing signing her name. Except she's signing it 'Lindsay Kent.' " Ryan sounds a little embarrassed.

Geez. My sister is a dork.

"You don't think Peg Leg got her?" Samir asks.

"There's no such thing as Peg Leg," Blade says. "Besides, I thought we agreed it was Ahab."

"Do you see anything else?" I shout.

"No," Ryan says. "There seem to be some footprints, though. And what looks like a cave, maybe. I'm not sure. I'm going to have to go look. You guys stay there, I'll be back."

Ryan disappears again.

"I guess we just have to wait for him," I say. I wish for the hundredth time that Heathcliff was here.

I hope he's okay.

Hana and Samir are sitting on a fallen tree. Blade sits down in a patch of grass and I lean against a tree stump.

"You guys think Heathcliff is in trouble?" I ask them.

"Heathcliff is probably eating a Big Mac at the nearest McDonald's. He's no fool," Samir says.

"Technically, he wouldn't know what one is," Blade says. "They didn't have Mickey D's in 1847."

"Details, details," Samir says, waving his hand. "By the way, what is edible around here? Isn't that supposed to be part of your witch training?"

"We're taught how to do spells, not how to forage for berries," Blade says.

The drums start up suddenly again, causing us all to jump. They're louder than ever and coming from down below, where Ryan disappeared.

"You hear that?" Samir whispers.

"You'd have to be deaf not to," Hana says.

"You think that means Ryan's in trouble?" I ask.

Back behind us, in the forest, we hear the sounds of branches cracking under feet. Samir jumps, everyone else stiffens.

"Maybe it means *we're* in trouble," Hana says.

"Maybe it's just Heathcliff?" I ask, even as more branches crack to our left, then others to our right. There isn't just one person coming our way. There are at least three or more. We start to hear the distinct grumble of voices. Men's voices.

"What do we do?" Samir hisses at us.

"Hide," Blade whispers back.

Twenty-one

Samir and Hana jump behind a big tree trunk, Blade crawls into the hallowed-out log, and I'm left to hide myself behind some bushes. My breath nearly stops as I get hit by a serious fit of déjà vu. I realize that this is the *exact* spot I dreamed about the night before. The bushes, the footsteps, everything. As the footsteps get closer, I suck in a breath and hold it.

The crack of branches comes closer and I hear the crunch of leaves under someone's feet.

A shadow crosses over my head and I freeze, peering out through the brush. I hope I don't see Peg Leg like I did in my dream. And then, in front of me, I see one dark bare leg and then another. Whoever is standing in front of me is barefoot, and he has spiral tattoos on his ankles.

I'm almost certain now that he sees me. I glance through a hole in the bushes and see that Hana is crouched opposite me in her hiding space. She sees that I'm about to be caught and I can tell she's going to do something silly.

She starts to stand up, even as I shake my head vigorously *no*. She shouldn't sacrifice herself for me. But then, she's already doing it.

"Hey, you! Over here!" she cries, jumping out from her hiding spot and drawing the man away from me. Before I can do a thing about it, the tattoo guy is off, running toward her, and she takes off at a sprint straight into the woods. I pop up from my hiding place, but it's too late to distract Tattoo Man. He's thumping off through the forest after Hana. I get a glimpse of his back. He's wearing what amounts to rags and has a completely bald head.

"Hana!" I shout, but Blade and Samir grab me before I can take off after her.

"Shhhhhh!" Blade says, covering my mouth with her hand. "Listen," she whispers.

I realize then that we're not alone. Tattoo Man wasn't alone, either, because his friends are coming at us through the woods. All I see are shadow figures, making their way through the trees.

"We're trapped," Samir whines.

"We've got only one way to go," Blade says, glancing over the cliff. "Down."

"We can't leave Hana," I say.

"We have to!" Blade shouts, as she slings her backpack

over her shoulder. Then she grabs a root hanging out from the cliff and starts to rappel down the muddy ledge.

"I don't know how to climb," Samir says.

"Neither do I," I say.

We both look at each other and then at the trees in front of us. Two pirate men break through. They're just like the ones I saw in the woods with Heathcliff. They're wearing rags and no shoes.

"You want to fight them or you want to climb?" I ask Samir as I scramble down after Blade, who I see is nearly halfway down the cliff face.

"Climb—definitely climb," Samir says, crossing himself even though he isn't Catholic before scrambling down the cliff. He's so scared that he passes by Blade and me, scooting in his haste to get down the side.

"Don't look down," Blade warns me, which of course makes me want to look down, and I do. It seems like I'm dangling at the top of a ten-story building. Below, all I can see is what looks like big rocks and some sand. If I fall, I know I'll hit the rocks.

"Ugh," I say, squeezing my eyes shut as my stomach does somersaults.

"I told you not to look down," Blade says.

A bit of dirt hits the top of my head. I look up and see the two men are crawling after us.

"Pirates!" Samir shouts, panicked. "Peg Leg! Pirates! Aaaaaaaaah!"

The pirates Samir is referring to are about six feet from us. One of them leans over and tries to swipe at us, but we're too far.

I scurry downward faster and lose my footing.

"Agh!" I say, my stomach flipping into my throat as I desperately claw at the side of the hill, hoping to find any kind of traction. I slide for what seems like forever before I finally grab hold of a root. I cling to it, feeling it slice into my palms. Serious ouch.

"Are you okay?" Blade shouts down to me. I look up at her and nod. Below me, Samir is nearly to the ground. Another clump of mud hits my head. I shake it off and look above me, seeing that the two pirates are gaining on us. Uh-oh. That's no good.

Even worse, my root is breaking. It's literally tearing as I cling to it. I'm still a good twenty feet from the ground and I'm about to lose my only grip on the cliff. I try to reach for another root, but it's too far. I'm in trouble. Big trouble.

And then, without any more warning, the root snaps completely and I'm free-falling again, arms and legs flailing against the side of the cliff. I squeeze my eyes shut, bracing for impact with the ground below, but instead my butt lands on something hard but soft. I open one eye to see that I've been caught. By Heathcliff.

"Where have you been?" I ask him.

"You mean aside from saving you—*again*?" Heathcliff

asks, quirking one eyebrow. I have to smile at this. He's not wrong. He puts me down, just as Blade finishes her descent. As I knock the mud and dirt off my plaid Bard uniform skirt and inspect myself for cuts and scrapes (I have more than I can count), Heathcliff takes off his Bard blazer and prepares to face the two island people. They, however, don't seem in any hurry to fight Heathcliff. In fact, their eyes grow wide in fear as they seem to recognize him from somewhere else. Both men start scrambling back up the cliff and, before I know it, they've scurried up and over the edge, disappearing back into the trees.

"Your reputation precedes you," Blade says.

"You are seriously the coolest guy ever," Samir says, putting up a high five. When Heathcliff gives him a look and doesn't return the five, Samir quickly drops his hand. "And way too cool for high fives even. Right. I forgot."

I'm suddenly aware that I'm with Heathcliff and I probably look like a wrinkled, crumpled mess after my little mountain-climbing stunt. Not to mention, having slept in my soggy Bard uniform probably did no favors for me nor my hair. But Heathcliff doesn't seem to care. He just gives me a warm smile.

"Did you see Ryan?" Samir asks. "He came down this way."

"No, but I may have found Lindsay," Heathcliff says, holding up her retainer.

Twenty-two

"Where did you get this?" I ask, yanking Lindsay's retainer from Heathcliff's hand. It's all bent, like someone's stepped on it. Not good. Not good at all. "Did you see her? Is she okay?"

"I don't know," Heathcliff says. "I didn't see her, but I think I know where they might be keeping her."

"Who's 'they'? Who has her? We have to find her!" I'm definitely starting to panic a little now.

"Calm down. We will," Heathcliff says, gently touching my arm.

"Where did you go anyway?" Blade asks him. "You missed all kinds of drama."

"Two men jumped me, taking me by surprise in the forest. They knocked me unconscious and carried me there." Heathcliff points out to the beach. "I think they're the same men who took Lindsay since I found her, uh, what do you call this?" He studies it like it's a dissected frog.

"Retainer," I tell him.

I can't help but think that she'd never let anyone take her retainer, at least not voluntarily. Lindsay's in serious trouble and this is all my fault. If I hadn't pushed her away and been such a lousy sister, she never would've listened to Parker in the first place. If anything happens to her, I won't forgive myself. I just won't.

"We should head this way," he says, taking me by the arm. Heathcliff pushes away some bramble and brush and the woods open up to a huge rocky beach. For a second, I take in the view, which is actually pretty amazing. Big ocean waves crash on the rocky beach, and as far as the eye can see there's just big blue ocean. A strong cold wind comes off the surf, blowing my hair back. Far in the distance, along the coast, I can see a tiny white dot—the lighthouse, which marks the spot where the Bard Academy ferry usually drops off students for the year. This beach, made mostly of rocks, looks completely deserted.

"Whoa," Samir says, standing next to me.

"It's water and rocks, what's the big deal?" Blade doesn't seem impressed. Then again, things not occult related don't do much for my former roomie.

"Footprints," Samir says, pointing down. "They must be Ryan's."

Heathcliff scowls. "Come on, we don't have time to lose."

Up close, the beach is even rockier than I thought. It's littered with giant gray boulders and it's not so easy to get around them. I slip more than once, but Heathcliff catches me, grabbing my arm or hand each time. The wind off the ocean is cold and pierces right through my thin Bard jacket. My hands feel raw and red from the cold and from the scrapes I got on the mountain.

I can't see much ahead because there are too many rocks in the way. As far as I can see, there's just another cliff face, this one all rock and no mud.

"Not much farther," Heathcliff tells us.

We make our way around another series of giant rocks and then, appearing before us, is a giant cave mouth, black and dark and gaping. Even stranger, it seems like the mouth of the cave is naturally in the form of a jagged whale's tail.

"Whale Cove," Samir breathes.

"Come on," Heathcliff says, tugging at my hand.

"We're going *in* there?" Samir asks. "But it's pitch-black."

"We have to go," Blade says. "Come on, I'll hold your hand, 'fraidy cat."

Samir and Blade exchange a long look. There is most definitely something going on between those two. She was all over him sophomore year, but then she started dating a basketball player and forgot about Samir altogether. Personally, I always thought Samir and Hana would hook up, although they bitterly deny any mutual attraction. Still, if Blade's interested in Samir again, that will definitely make things in our little friend circle more interesting.

Of course, thinking about Hana makes me wonder if she's okay.

"Guys, you think Hana escaped?" I ask them.

Blade and Samir send me a guilty look. Apparently, neither one of them had been thinking of her.

"I'm sure she's fine," Samir says quickly.

"Oh yeah, definitely," Blade says.

I really hope they're right. I don't have much time to dwell on Hana because we're now walking along a very narrow, rocky path leading inside the cave. When the waves crash on the rocks nearby we get splashed with spray. Above our heads, giant stalactites drip salty water and the whole place smells like salt water and brine. High above our heads I see the flicker of tiny creatures with wings.

"Birds?" Samir asks, hopeful.

"No, even better—bats," Blade says, looking up.

And then, before we make it too far, something white and sticky drops on Samir's shoulder.

"Gross!" he says, trying to wipe his sleeve on a nearby rock wall.

"Bat droppings are supposed to make good love potions," Blade says.

"And that's supposed to make me feel better how?" Samir asks her.

Heathcliff flicks open his lighter and the flame casts an eerie glow around the cave. He leads the way down the narrow path and all I can hear are the sounds of water splashing against the rocks and the shuffle of Samir's feet behind me. We walk for a few minutes, the cave yawning above our heads, the flittering wings of bats casting shadows on the ceiling.

Up ahead, I see a dim light. As soon as Heathcliff sees it, he shuts off his lighter. He gives us a low shush sound, telling us to be quiet. We creep forward a few more paces, turning a sharp corner, and Heathcliff signals us to duck down. We do, following him as he crawls up to a big boulder and hunches down behind it. I put myself next to Heathcliff, my hand on his back to steady myself, and peer around it to see what he's seeing.

There are torches on the walls, which explains the light, but there's more. Much more.

At first I blink, not quite believing my eyes. There, in the shallow waters of the enclosed cove, there's a giant ship. I don't know for sure, but it looks like a pirate ship. It has vast sails and old wood, and it's lurching a little to the right. It's tall, so tall that the top mast nearly touches the ceiling of the cave.

And there, on the side of the ship, are the unmistakable letters:

PEQUOD.

"It's the ship from *Moby-Dick,*" I hiss, nudging Blade and Samir. "Hana was right. It *was* Ahab who was following us."

"Since when do you read?" Blade asks me.

"Since I had to work in my stepmom's shop all summer," I say.

"Whoa. You think someone managed to summon an *entire ship* from fiction?" Samir asks, a little in awe. "That means the pirates . . ."

"Are really a whaling crew," Blade finishes.

"Shhhhh," Heathcliff breathes, putting his hand out to us. We peer around the rock and see that we're not alone. A few of the crew are milling about on the deck of the ship, which is lighted from within. A yellow glow seeps out of the windows near the stern.

"Since when do whalers kidnap random students?" Samir asks. "That never happened in the book."

"I don't know," I say. "But those are definitely the men I saw in the woods near Bard."

I'd recognize the toothless one, who chased Heathcliff and me, anywhere. But I notice that I don't see any of the men who chased us down the cliff.

We watch as they descend a rope ladder along the side and jump to the ground. They dust off their hands and then head toward us. We all duck down.

I wait, without breathing, as the crew members shuffle past us and out the other side of the cave opening. We wait a good two or three minutes and then Heathcliff pops his head up and looks around.

"Come on," he tells us.

We follow him to the ship, glancing over our shoulders as if fearing the sudden appearance of Ahab.

"How do you know there're not more crew members on the boat?" Samir whispers to Heathcliff.

"I don't," Heathcliff says as he grabs hold of the rope ladder and begins climbing upward. Blade and I follow.

"Why am I not filled with confidence right now?" Samir asks as he joins Blade and me on the rope ladder.

It's a lot harder to climb than it looks and with the four of us on it, there's some serious swaying going on. Not to mention, the boat is seriously huge. We're talking three stories of climbing.

Heathcliff makes it to the top first and crawls up. I hear the thump of his shoes on the deck. I can sense he's checking things out and then I see his head pop over the side.

"All clear," he says, holding out his hand and helping me over the wooden railing. Blade and Samir follow and the three of us find ourselves on the deck of the *Pequod.*

"It's bigger than I thought," Samir says. "In the book, I thought it would be smaller."

"It's got to carry a whale carcass, remember?" I say.

"Well, I certainly don't want to run into the whale then, if it's bigger than this ship," Samir says.

We take a few more steps and see there are several Bard students in muddied uniforms tied to the main mast, but neither one is Parker or Ryan. I nudge Heathcliff and together we go over and untie them.

"Dude, thanks!" says the guy I recognize from the woods, the first one to be taken.

"Have you seen a girl? Her name is Lindsay and she's my sister." I wish I had a picture to show them, but I don't.

"Did she have a limp?" one of the other guys asks.

I realize I don't know. She could've hurt herself—or been hurt by someone else.

"No, dude, that girl was Parker Rodham," the shaggy-hair guy says.

"Parker is here?" Blade asks.

"Yeah, along with some other dude," he says. "They're downstairs or something.

You know they're just holding her for ransom. Her

dad is supposed to be loaded. I don't know why they bothered with us, we're financial aid kids."

"You think Lindsay could be downstairs?" I ask Heathcliff, who nods.

"Listen, we'd love to stay and help, but we've had enough of this freak show." The shaggy-haired guy, now free, is inching his way over to the side of the ship.

"Yeah, especially Long John Silver, or whoever the wooden leg guy is," another says.

"You saw a guy with a wooden leg?" Samir asks, starting to get nervous.

"Yeah, and he's freakin' crazy, dude," the guy answers. "If you know what's good for you, you'll get out of here, too."

"We can't, not until we find my sister," I say.

"Suit yourself," the shaggy-haired guy says and then he and the others slip over the side of the ship.

"Shouldn't someone go with them? You know, make sure they get back to campus safely?" Samir asks, hopeful.

Blade and I give him disapproving looks. He shrugs. "Can't blame a guy for trying," he says.

"This way," Heathcliff interrupts, leading us down a short flight of stairs on deck, toward the flickering light below. Beneath our feet, the deck creaks and moans a little. It's moored in the relatively shallow waters of the cove, but it's still afloat. There's the slightest suggestion of swaying back and forth. Every so often I hear the wooden mast groan under the weight of the sails.

"Creepy," I say.

"Yeah," Blade says, sounding a little too happy about it.

We fall silent as the passageway in front of us narrows and grows darker. Up ahead, there's a door. Heathcliff tries it once, but finds it locked.

"Hang on, this is my department," Blade says, inching forward. She drops to her knees and grabs a black bobby pin from her hair. Blade got in trouble back home for breaking into her neighbor's garage and stealing his lawn gnomes. Lock picking is her forte. After a few minutes of struggling, she has the lock open. "I would've been faster, but I'm not an antiques expert," she explains.

The door creaks open and inside I see Ryan and Parker, both tied up, seated back to back in chairs. They're both gagged. Seeing us, their eyes grow wide and they try to tell us something, but it all just comes out as muffled murmurs. I grab Ryan's gag and pull it down.

"Thank God," he says. "These people are crazy. They're taking the Peg Leg story way too seriously."

Parker is squirming and fighting her ropes. Is it bad

that I don't want to remove her gag just yet? Once freed, though, she actually looks grateful.

"Thank God," she sighs, real relief in her eyes. "I thought I was going to be cut up with a rusty saw or something. You know, it's always the pretty girls who get the gruesome deaths in horror movies. And I have to say, I am *so* sorry I even mentioned Peg Leg."

"He says he's Ahab, technically," Ryan corrects, giving me a sheepish glance.

"Ahab—you're sure?" I ask him. So Hana was right. Peg leg *is* Ahab. But then, who else would be at the helm of the *Pequod*? I look at Ryan. "Does that mean you're starting to believe me?"

"There still could be a rational explanation," he mutters, not meeting my eyes.

Unbelievable. Even after coming face-to-face with Ahab and the *Pequod,* Ryan is still skeptical. What will it take to make him believe?

Out of the corner of my eye I see Heathcliff frown. He's not happy that we found Ryan or that I'm talking to him.

"I'd love to hear the explanation of this ship, then," Blade says as she and Samir work to loosen their ropes.

"But where's Lindsay?" Heathcliff asks, eyes narrow. "She was with you, wasn't she?"

"No," Ryan says, shaking his head. "We haven't seen her." He sends me a sympathetic glance. "I'm sorry, Miranda. I don't know where she is. Or if . . ." He deliberately trails off.

"Or if what?"

"If Ahab may have hurt her. He was talking about giving us thirty lashes for insubordination. He thinks we're members of his crew," Ryan finishes.

Thirty lashes? Like with a whip? I swallow, hard. Lindsay may be a pain in the butt, but she doesn't deserve that. God, I hope she's okay.

Blade finishes loosening Ryan's ropes when we hear clumping sounds against the wooden boards above our heads, like someone is walking on the deck above us. Several someones. And then an odd knocking sound against the deck, like someone banging a broom handle against the wooden boards.

"Ahab," Ryan whispers to us.

The boards above our heads creak, with a thump and a knock—*thump, knock, thump, knock*—as Ahab makes his way over the deck. By now, he's probably discovered some of his captives have escaped.

We're all silent, even as Heathcliff scans the room for exits. There's only one, the narrow passageway that will take us to the stairs, straight up to the deck. We all look at one another and then draw the same conclusion—it's better to risk the stairs than be caught in close quarters. Samir and Blade head out first, followed by Parker and Ryan. I'm behind them and Heathcliff trails last. We creep together out the narrow hall, lighted only by the flicker of oil lanterns. Beneath our feet, the boat sways a little in the water, and I have to put my hand to the wall to steady myself. Ahead, I can see Blade and Samir tentatively climbing the stairs, with Ryan and Parker waiting their turn.

"Hurry *up,*" Parker hisses at Samir, who is taking longer than usual to get up the ladder. I don't blame him. I wouldn't want to dash up the stairs, either, in case Ahab is waiting above.

Blade and Samir reach the deck without incident, it seems, and Ryan and Parker follow them. It's my turn next and I follow them, creeping slowly up the ladder. There's no sign of Ahab yet, or his men, as we make our way back to the rope ladder on the side of the ship. But when we get there, there's no rope ladder. Someone's reeled it in.

I turn around just in time to realize it's a trap. Ahab, with his peg leg, steps out on the deck, and he's soon joined by several members of his crew, who material-ize from various hiding places on the ship.

"You're just in time," Ahab says, a slow smile creep-ing across his face. "We set sail shortly. In the mean-time, men, *restrain our guests.*"

Twenty-three

Parker doesn't wait to hear what else Ahab has to say, she simply bolts away from him toward the back of the ship. Ryan stays with us. He and Heathcliff square off against some of Ahab's men.

One of them jumps on Heathcliff and another threatens to take me, but Ryan leaps in front and takes on the sailor before he can. Blade tackles yet another sailor and starts pounding on his back, while Samir grabs a nearby harpoon strapped against the ship's mast and throws one to me. I use mine to knock off the crew member hanging on Heathcliff's back. Now free, Heathcliff grabs the harpoon and then shoves me roughly behind him, protecting me from the other four advancing crew members. Out of the corner of my eye, I see Parker get grabbed from behind by a sailor just before she makes it to the railing. She struggles and shouts Ryan's name. Instantly, Ryan turns and runs to help her. I don't have time to dwell on the Ryan-Parker connection because I'm busy ducking another sailor, who's wearing an eye patch and comes at me with his arms swinging. Heathcliff, however, makes short work of him.

I hear a scream and I look up just in time to see Parker flung to the ground. Ryan tries to help her, but he, too, is taken, and the two of them struggle as the sailors tie them to the main mast on deck with thick, wide ropes. Blade and Samir aren't faring much better as they try to fend off two more sailors and, even worse, there are more crew members pouring out from doors and hatches on the ship. Pretty soon, we'll be completely swamped.

Heathcliff, seeing that we'll soon be surrounded, grabs my hand and pulls me toward the mast. He's already got one foot on a peg sticking out of the wood. He plans to climb.

"Wait, what about them?" I ask, pointing to Samir and Blade. "We have to help them."

"We're no good to them captured," Heathcliff tells me. "We have to climb," he adds, shoving me up ahead of him. There are foot and hand holds that I grab on to and, before I can think about it, I'm climbing frantically upward.

"What are we doing?" I ask as the people below us become smaller and smaller. Below me, Heathcliff kicks at a sailor who tries to follow us. He falls back down about ten feet, landing on the deck.

"Just go!" he tells me.

I glance down in time to see that Samir has been captured and so has Blade. Both are struggling fiercely against their captors, but they've been overwhelmed. I watch as sailors take them belowdecks. Parker and Ryan are now completely tied up against the main mast.

Heathcliff has one hand around the harpoon he's used as a weapon and the other grasping the handholds on the mast.

Soon I run out of places to climb, finding myself at the top of the mast, where I pull myself into a small lookout station—a round half barrel only big enough for one person. I scoot to the edge, but there's no room for Heathcliff. He holds on to the rail and looks down, seeing that we're being pursued by three more crew members.

"What now?"

Heathcliff says nothing, just whips around quickly, looking for ideas.

"Um, I think we ought to figure something out, and fast," I say. The crew members are gaining on us and more have joined the chase upward. I don't know if Heathcliff can take them all. The deck looms far below us, and if we fell, we'd both be dead, no question.

Heathcliff grabs the end of a rope, which is lying on the lookout post. The other end is attached to the huge sail, about ten feet from us. He stands me up.

"Hold on to me," he commands, and I loop my arms around his neck so that I'm hanging on his back.

I don't have time to even speak. Heathcliff swings us out onto the rope, away from the mast where the crewmembers are climbing, and we fly straight into the open sail. Before I can figure out what's happening, we're zooming downward. The rope we're clinging to is bringing up the sail in front of us like a window shade. We zip down, straight past the crew members, and land with a *thump* on the wooden deck.

But before we can make it to the side of the ship, three of Ahab's men jump us. Heathcliff easily throws one overboard, but finds himself tangled up with the second. I'm struggling with the third. Before I know it, he's somehow gotten ahold of my locket, *Heathcliff's* locket, and ripped it straight from my neck.

"What's this, eh?" says the crew member, holding me apart with one hand while he examines the gold locket. With a flick of his finger, he's opened it, and the tiny piece of paper within it—the single thing holding Heathcliff to this world—flitters out.

"No!" I shout, wrenching loose from the sailor's grasp and diving for the piece of paper as it flutters to the ground. But it escapes me, born up by the wind, and flies just out of my grasp. I lunge for it again, only to have it stepped on by a wooden peg.

I look up and see that the peg leg belongs, of course, to Ahab.

He reaches down and peels the piece of paper from under the wooden peg.

"No, wait, I need that . . ."

"You do, do you?" he says, giving me a smile. An evil smile.

"I'll take that," comes a woman's voice from somewhere behind the throng of sailors. It sounds familiar. I crane to see.

Then, before my eyes, Ms. P steps forward through the group. I can't believe it. It's Ms. P, Sylvia Plath's ghost, from campus.

"Give it to me," she commands Ahab. He does what she says.

"Ms. P! You have to help us. Ahab and . . ." I sputter.

"I know," she says, nodding slowly.

"You have to stop him," I say, but she doesn't look like she intends to stop Ahab or anyone else. In fact, she looks bemused.

"You're not here to rescue us, are you?"

"I'm afraid not, my dear," Ms. P says, shaking her head slowly. She shows me a book. It's the original copy of *Moby-Dick*. The magic copy from the vault. The one she used to conjure up Ahab, his crew, and this ship.

I glance over to my right. Parker and Ryan are watching, confused.

"But why?" I ask Ms. P.

"Why?" Her hand slips into her pocket and pulls out the small framed picture of her children. "Do you even know what it's like to be without your children for eternity? It's torture. I *have* to see them again."

I can feel Ryan's eyes on me and Ms. P. He's taking it in. Maybe *now* he'll believe me.

"Maybe we can find another way," I tell her, feeling a little sad for her. She's clearly desperate to see them again. "A safer way. Maybe with Ms. W's help we could—"

"Forget it," Ms. P says. "I've found a way."

She slips the photo back into her pocket. As she does, her glance slips away from mine and I see my chance. It's now or never. I leap for Ms. P, trying to aim for the book in her hand and the slip of paper from *Wuthering Heights*.

Of course, no sooner than I jump, I find myself frozen in midleap. What the . . . ?

"You didn't *really* think I'd let you take this book?" Ms. P says, holding her arm outstretched to me. She's holding me somehow, making sure I can't move. I struggle, but it's no use. I kick my legs, but I'm struggling against air.

"Let her go," Heathcliff growls, taking three steps toward Ms. P.

"I don't think I will," Ms. P says, examining the torn piece of paper in her hand. The last remaining bit of *Wuthering Heights.* "I think, Heathcliff, that you've far outworn your welcome here."

With that, she takes a nearby oil lantern, picks it up, and feeds the piece of paper into the top of it.

"No!" I scream as Heathcliff struggles against his captors. We both watch helplessly as the tiny piece of paper turns black in the small flame.

"Throw him overboard," Ms. P commands.

"Heathcliff—no! Wait!" I shout, struggling against the man who holds me.

Heathcliff meets my eyes. He looks resigned to his fate. He mouths three words to me.

"I love you."

The tears start to roll down my face and a sob escapes my throat. I strain against Ms. P's invisible grip, but I can't move. I'm held fast.

As I watch, helpless, strong hands shove Heathcliff backward and he falls headfirst over the side of the boat. I strain to hear a splash, anything that might signal that he made it to the cove waters below, but I hear nothing.

I can't help but think it's because he disappeared before he made it to the water. He's been sent back to *Wuthering Heights.*

And just like that, he's gone.

I'm sobbing now, even as Ms. P releases her grip and I hit the deck, hard.

"How could you do that?" I shout at Ms. P.

"How could I *not* do that? I have plans, Miranda, and Heathcliff isn't in them. Besides, he's a terrible brute, don't you know? Or didn't you read *Wuthering Heights*?"

My chest feels like it's been torn in two. Parker and Ryan are still watching, but I don't care anymore. I don't care if Ryan believes me. I don't care about anything.

"Now, Ahab, let's set sail," Ms. P says.

Ahab turns to the men around him and shouts, "Men, we sail for the white whale! We find the white whale and we go home!"

A shout goes up from the crew.

"You won't get away with this," I tell Ms. P, anger bubbling up in me.

"And who's going to stop me?" Ms. P asks. "Now, tie her up and take her down below."

Twenty-four

"Now what?" Blade asks as she and Samir struggle against their ropes. We're all tied, back-to-back in chairs, in the cargo hold. Parker and Ryan are with us, too. Ms. P ordered all of us belowdecks so that the rest of the crew could get ready to sail.

Ryan's hands are touching mine, bound together by the same rope. Not that I feel them. I don't feel anything. I'm numb all over. There's only one thought in my head: Heathcliff is gone. Forever.

"We've got to find a way out of here, for starters," Samir says.

"Um, no duh," Blade says. "I was hoping for more of a concrete suggestion."

"Why isn't anyone talking about how Ms. P just levitated Miranda?" Parker asks. "Is no one else freaked out by that? I mean—hello! *Mindfreak,* special!"

"Miranda, I should've believed you," Ryan is saying

next to me. "I'm sorry. I see that you really were trying to tell me something real."

"Believed what? Will *someone* fill me in?" Parker demands.

Everyone ignores her.

"Miranda?" Ryan asks, nudging me gently. "Say something."

I don't answer him. I feel dead inside. Heathcliff is gone and everything seems completely hopeless. What's the point of explaining things to Ryan? What's the point of anything?

"Miranda?" Ryan tries again.

"Don't bother. She's heartbroken, or can't you tell?" Blade says.

Ryan flinches. "I don't understand," he says.

"Sorry to be the one to break this to you, pal," Samir says, "but she's had a thing for Heathcliff since day one."

"She's only had the hots for him forever," Blade agrees. "And now he's gone. Poof. Back to *Wuthering Heights*."

"Wuthering Heights? What the hell is everyone talking about?" Parker asks, sounding even more annoyed.

I can barely even hear what anyone is saying. My life is over. I didn't realize how much Heathcliff really meant to me until now. Now that I can't even see him again.

"Is this true, Miranda?" Ryan asks me, eyes imploring and demanding an answer.

I glance up at him. I know I owe him an explanation. I should tell him something, anything, but I just can't. I'm too far gone. Nothing seems to matter anymore. What good would explaining do? Heathcliff is gone and there's nothing that will change that.

"Just let Miranda have a quiet minute, okay? She's been through a lot," Blade says. Ryan drops the conversation. Apparently, the look on my face told him everything he wanted to know.

"I hate to interrupt this little love triangle, but will *someone* tell me what the hell is happening around here?" Parker demands.

"Should we tell her?" Samir asks Blade.

Blade narrows her eyes. The thought doesn't appeal to her. "I don't know if Parker can *handle* the truth."

"If *someone* doesn't tell me what is going on right now, I'm going to scream," Parker says.

"Let's just tell her. I've got a headache already and screaming won't help," Samir says.

"Fine, but you do it." Blade says. "I'm not doing that skank any favors."

"Who are you calling a skank, you freak?"

"You want to know what's going on or not?" Samir asks.

"Just get on with it, already," Parker mutters.

"Okay, check this," Samir says, then takes a deep breath. In a rapid-fire speed voice he starts explaining, "We're trapped on the ship from *Moby-Dick* with crazy Ahab as the captain. He's doing the bidding of Ms. P, who is really Sylvia Plath's ghost, because all the Bard faculty are actually dead—it's purgatory!—and she's trying to escape, which might be impossible without actually destroying the world and/or universe. Special books in the vault beneath the school contain the souls of all the teachers and can bring fictional characters to life like our friend Ahab and recently banished Heathcliff. And we all know this because we're part of the Literary Investigative Team—name courtesy of Blade—and we pretty much save the world every semester." Samir takes in a deep breath. "Whew. Did I leave anything out?" he asks Blade.

"That pretty much covers it," Blade says. "But just because you know this doesn't mean you get a LITs T-shirt," she warns Parker.

"Uh-huh, right," Parker says. "Do you think I'm an idiot?"

"Is that a serious question or a rhetorical one?" Samir asks. "Because I've definitely got an answer for you."

"Quit joking around," she says, sounding seriously annoyed. "Would someone please tell me what's *really* going on?"

"Such a nonbeliever," Blade says.

"It's sad, really," Samir agrees.

"You guys are insane," Parker declares.

"How else do you think Ms. P levitated Miranda?" Blade says. "You saw it. She's a ghost. Deal with it."

"That's ridiculous," Parker says. "I don't believe . . ."

I hear a massive churning sound, like metal on metal, and realize that a group of sailors on the other side of the ship are hoisting up the anchor. Within seconds, the deck beneath our feet shifts and suddenly we're moving toward the opening of the cave. In seconds, bright daylight blinds us as the ship sails free of the cove. The tide is taking us out.

"Are we moving? We're totally moving," Samir says.

"That's what ships do," Blade says.

"I *told* you guys this would happen," Samir frets. "We're going out to sea! Oh my God, I can't swim!"

"As long as we're on the ship, you won't have to," Blade points out. "Do you think Ms. P can really sail out of purgatory? I mean, is that possible?"

"How should I know?" Samir says.

"Still going on about purgatory!" Parker sniffs. "Ha!"

"Shut up, Parker," Ryan snaps.

"Oh, come on, you don't *really* believe all this?" Parker huffs.

The ship shudders and groans beneath our feet. It's headed out to sea.

"But how did she conjure up all of this by herself?" Blade says, ignoring Parker and Ryan. "I didn't think ghosts could do it on their own, and not to mention something this big? A ship?"

"She had to have help," I say, speaking for the first time. I'm starting to come out of my fog a little. There's something about this whole situation that bothers me. Something I'm missing.

"Whatever, you *all* are certifiable," Parker says.

"Parker, if you aren't going to help, just be quiet," Ryan says.

"That's the best suggestion I've heard all day," Blade says.

"Shhhhh," I hiss. "I think I hear something."

"Hear what?"

"Listen."

In the hall there are voices. Heated voices. Both female.

"You promised I'd get to have him!"

"In time, dear. In good time."

"But you *promised.*"

That whine is unmistakable. Lindsay! And she's arguing with Ms. P.

"Is that who I think it is?" Blade asks me.

"Shhhh. I can't hear."

"I told you I would help you, but *only* if you got Ryan for me," Lindsay says. She stomps her foot because now she's pouting. "But you won't even let me see him."

"Lindsay! Is that you? Are you okay?" I shout.

"Miranda? What are *you* doing here?" Lindsay cries, coming into the cargo hold with Ms. P trailing behind.

I blink fast. She's okay and in one piece, but she's not tied up, and she doesn't seem to be Ms. P's prisoner. Wait, I'm confused. She's *not* a prisoner after all?

"Trying to save you, Einstein," Blade says.

"What do I need saving from?" Lindsay asks, looking confused.

"These sailors didn't take you hostage?" Samir asks.

"Hardly!" Lindsay snorts. She's finding this all very funny. "Ms. P told me I'd get extra credit if I came out here and helped her. She said I couldn't do it, but I totally proved her wrong."

"So Parker wasn't the one who dared you to find Whale Cove?" I ask, the truth starting to sink in.

"*Pffft,*" Lindsay says, shaking her head. "No."

"I *told* you," Parker says. "But you wouldn't listen to me!"

It all becomes clear to me at once. Of course—my sister is part fiction, like I am. She's got special powers in this place, too, and Ms. P has harnessed them to help her in her scheme. And Lindsay has no idea she's playing with fire. Lindsay is probably the one who helped her bring the ship to life. Lindsay is Ms. P's partner in crime.

"Ryan! There you are," Lindsay says, seeing Ryan for the first time. "Why is he tied up?" she asks Ms. P. "Untie him!"

"In good time," Ms. P says.

"Lindsay, you've got to stop helping Ms. P," I say, trying again. "What you're doing—bringing these fictional characters to life—is really bad news. It'll make the dimensions unstable. You could cause the end of the world."

"Blah, blah, blah. Whatever. Ms. P says that's all baloney."

"That's right, Lindsay," Ms. P purrs. "Your sister just wants to keep you from being great. She's just jealous that you are more powerful than she is."

"I am not! Lindsay, I swear, this is serious. You have to stop playing around."

"Don't talk to me like that," Lindsay says. "I'm not a child, okay? And you're not my mother, so quit acting like it."

"Okay, girl, seriously?" Blade says. "Miranda isn't fooling. She's telling the truth. You could totally end us all right now."

Lindsay considers Blade for a second, then dismisses her. "You're just saying that because you're her friend."

"Um, Lindsay. We're all tied up. Do you wanna ask Ms. P why we're all tied up?" Samir asks. "Ryan? A little help here."

Ryan swivels his head around. "Lindsay, it's true. You've got to stop."

"Um, and I don't know what anybody here is talking about," Parker says, "but Lindsay, if you don't untie us *right now,* I am going to make sure you're a social pariah on campus and that *no one* ever talks to you *ever* again."

"Enough," Ms. P says. "Don't worry about Parker, Lindsay, and Ryan is just saying that because he's still in love with your sister. Your sister is trying to steal him from you!"

"Lindsay, I'm not, I swear," I say. And I realize it's completely true. It's then that I realize that despite Ryan's gorgeousness, I really am over him. He's like a good friend, nothing more. It's Heathcliff I really love. And he's the one who's gone forever.

Lindsay seems to consider this a moment. I decide to take another stab at convincing her that Ms. P is crazy. "And why don't you ask Ms. P why she's been kidnapping students. That's not something a sane person does."

"We needed crew members," Ms. P says. "For the

ship. We had a little mutiny and we didn't have enough crew to sail."

"Mutiny?" I ask. "There's no mutiny in *Moby-Dick*. There's the threat of one, but it doesn't actually happen."

Ms. P throws back her head and laughs a little. "So, Headmaster Brontë didn't tell you that things don't always go according to plan? Not with fiction in this world. Anything can happen, but didn't you know that already? Once you release a story into the world it can take on new shapes. Like a mutiny. Or a car crash instead of a sinking boat, in Rebecca's case."

Ryan's head snaps up. "What did you say?"

How does Ms. P know about that, I wonder.

"It's of no matter," Ms. P adds mysteriously. "The important thing, Lindsay, is that only I can tell you about Bard's *real* secrets."

"Yeah, *real* secrets," Lindsay echoes.

"And you didn't trust her to tell her the truth to begin with," Ms. P adds. "Why on earth would Lindsay trust you now?"

"Yeah!" Lindsay seconds.

"Lindsay, shut up!" I can't stand it when she pretends to be a parrot. Immediately, I regret the outburst.

"Oh, I am *so* not doing you any favors now," Lindsay says, then sticks her tongue out at me.

"That's okay. I told Ms. W where we'd be," I say,

suddenly remembering the note I left. Surely she's found it by now. "When she finds you, she's going to totally put you on toilet duty."

"Ms. W?" Ms. P says, a small smile on her face. "You mean *this* Ms. W?" She lifts up a copy of Virginia Woolf's *To the Lighthouse*. It can only mean one thing. She's trapped Ms. W in her own book. And that means no one is coming to help us.

"You didn't!" I shout, tugging on my ropes.

"Come on, Lindsay, we have work to do," Ms. P says, guiding her to the stairs.

"Yeah, Ms. P and I are going to summon Moby Dick. Bet you never did anything like *that,*" Lindsay says.

"Moby Dick! Lindsay, you can't do that. He's huge. He'll . . ."

"End the world as we know it. Blah, blah. So you say!" Lindsay says, skipping up the stairs after Ms. P.

"We are *so* dead," Samir says after the two of them leave.

"Is your sister *always* like that?" Blade asks me.

"Pretty much," I say.

"So remind me again why we were doing the rescue thing?"

"I'm seriously beginning to forget now," I say.

"Maybe we can break free," Ryan says, struggling against the ropes. He pushes and tugs, but gets nowhere.

"You think you're going to get free that way? Please," Blade sniffs.

"You've got a better idea?"

"Maybe a rescue spell or something?" Samir asks Blade.

"I *told* you that witchcraft doesn't work that way. I could curse Lindsay, though."

"I could get behind that," I say.

"You guys are all certifiable, all of you," Parker says. "I still don't believe any of this crap."

"I hate to be a wet blanket, but could we focus on the escape part of the plan?" Samir asks.

"Maybe we can find something in here to cut the ropes with?" I ask.

"The only thing I see in here is gunpowder and whiskey," Ryan says, pointing to the barrels. "And maybe some stale crackers."

It's true that our surroundings are pretty bleak. Out our little round window, the sky seems to be getting darker, too. It looks like a storm is coming, which would explain why the floor beneath our feet seems to be swaying a little more forcefully than when we started this little trip. And the lanterns hooked into the ceiling are swinging back and forth. Our chairs, which aren't tied to anything except each other, start to slide a little.

"Whoa, did you do that?" I ask Samir.

"No. Did you?" he asks me.

"I wouldn't have asked you if I'd done it," I point out.

"Fair point," he says.

"Somebody better do something," Parker says. "I am not going out to sea. I get seasick."

"Um, guys, I think the wind is picking up," Blade says. "The waves are, too."

"We all have to work together," Ryan says, taking charge. You do have to admire his cool head in the face of what's likely to be total disaster. "If we all move together as one, maybe we can get closer to the stairs. I think there's a latch near the door. Maybe we could use it to cut the ropes."

Just as he finishes his sentence, our chairs slide even more, this time so much that I nearly topple into a barrel of gunpowder. Above our heads, a lantern swings dangerously high on its hook, sending darting shadows across the cargo hold. I hear shouting above deck.

"Let's move together, toward the staircase, on three," Ryan says.

We all struggle even harder against our ropes. Suddenly, the ship lurches violently to one side and our chairs topple over. Samir, Ryan, and Parker hit the deck hard with their shoulders. Blade and I are half-suspended in the air in our giant chair circle.

"Is everyone okay?" I ask.

"Easy for you to ask, given you're on top," Samir says. He's pinned to the ground with Ryan and Parker. Ryan grunts that he's okay. Parker shouts to all of us to get up and off her.

The ship lurches back the other way, sending us sliding on our sides back to our former position. The sudden change in direction knocks the lantern above our heads off its hook and onto the ground, where it bounces once, then rolls toward us, its safety latch flying open and its wick exposed just a few feet from us.

"That's not good," I say, noticing that the open flame is dangerously close to the barrels of gunpowder and whiskey all around us.

"Do you have any fire extinguisher spells there, Sabrina the Teenage Witch?" Samir asks Blade.

"Do I *look* like Melissa Joan Hart to you?" Blade spits. "Now, shut up and blow!"

Frantically, we start blowing in the direction of the lantern, hoping to put it out, but it's too far away.

"We've got to get closer," Ryan says. All together we try to wiggle our way closer, trying to kick against our ropes. But it's slow going, especially since Parker doesn't know how to work as part of a team. Her every movement seems to be going against the grain.

"Parker! Move with us!" I shout.

"I am!" she snaps back.

The flame grows bigger in front of our eyes, then the ship careens again to one side, sending the lantern rolling straight into a nearby burlap bag. The fire licks at the edges and it starts to smoke. Just inches from the sack, there's a wooden barrel full of black powder.

"Tell me that's not gunpowder," I say.

"And since when do we ever get a break? You know it's going to have the gunpowder," Samir says.

Right. Of course it is.

Twenty-five

"Blow harder!" Blade shouts at us, even though it's becoming pretty clear that we're not really doing much to stop the flames.

"You know, that sounds kind of dirty," Samir says.

"Just blow, perv!" Parker snaps.

"There's a little sawdust down here," Ryan says. "I'll try to kick some on the flames. Parker! Help me!"

"I'm trying!" she huffs. "I'm tied up, or didn't you notice?"

Frantically, we all work to stop the fire, but it's no use. There's not enough sawdust to suffocate the fire and blowing on it does absolutely no good. We watch helplessly as the fire travels up the burlap sack, getting even closer to the barrel of gunpowder sitting nearby.

Ryan struggles against the ropes, tugging and pulling with all his might.

"Fire! Fire!" Samir shouts. "Somebody help!"

"I don't think anyone is going to hear us," Blade says.

She's probably right. There is a huge storm outside *and* there's a giant whale attacking the ship. And yet, over the crackling sound of the fire, the lurching of the ship, and Samir's cries for help, I hear someone calling my name. It's faint at first, then it gets louder.

"Here! I'm in here!"

Before I know it, the door has swung open and there's a shadow of a figure standing there. A figure that looks a lot like . . .

"Heathcliff?" I ask, still not sure if I can believe my eyes.

It sure looks like him. Broad shoulders, dark, unreadable eyes, and his longish black hair that's wet from the storm outside and sticking to his forehead in curly clumps.

Relief floods over me. He didn't get zapped back to *Wuthering Heights.* He's here. He's really here!

He sweeps in and without hesitating, stomps on the fire with his boots. Then he suffocates the remaining flames with the wet Bard blazer he whips off his back. I can see the outline of his broad shoulders through his shirt. He wipes sweat and rain from his brow as he stomps the last flicker of a spark underneath his heel.

"But I thought you left," I manage to stutter. "Forever."

"Yeah, you were totally gone," Blade says.

"Poof! Into thin air," Samir adds. When Heathcliff frowns at him, Samir is quick to add, "Not, of course, that we're sorry to see you survived. I mean, obviously."

Ryan gives Heathcliff a long look, but says nothing.

"Whatever," Parker snaps. "Will you just untie us already? You won't believe what these losers have been saying about you. They think you're a fictional character."

Heathcliff says nothing, just goes about untying us silently.

"I mean, that's crazy. Tell them it's crazy," Parker says.

Heathcliff doesn't answer her and Parker starts to look a little unsettled.

"So are you going to tell us what the heck happened, or what?" Blade asks.

"I don't know," Heathcliff says, shrugging. "I fell into a boat tied along the side of the ship. I sat there thinking that I really didn't want to go back to *Wuthering Heights,* and I kept thinking about you."

He stares at me as he says this.

"And so I stayed," he adds, whipping the last bit of rope around my legs free.

Immediately, I spring up and throw my arms around him, tears blurring my vision.

"We've got to get out of here," Ryan interrupts. There's jealousy in his voice, and annoyance. If Parker notices, she doesn't let on. She's still trying to process the fact that Heathcliff is fictional. Heathcliff is not the kind of guy to make something like that up or to go along with a joke. She's clearly uneasy now. As I watch, she actually reaches up and touches Heathcliff's sleeve, as if to make sure he's actually real.

"Um, yeah," Samir says. "Could you guys save the romantic reunion for some other time? We've got a world to save and I'm still tied up here," Samir says, holding up his hands.

"Ditto," Blade says, raising hers.

No sooner than Heathcliff unties Blade and Samir, the ship lurches violently to one side again, sending all of us sprawling. I fall to the ground, landing hard on my knees. A barrel of gunpowder comes loose from its moorings and starts to roll straight for my head. I curl up in a protective ball, but Heathcliff is there, putting his body in between me and the barrel. It hits him hard, but he stops it.

"Are you okay?" I ask him.

"Fine," he groans, holding his side.

The ship lurches again, but we all manage to keep our footing. Ryan helps steady Parker.

"If I get out of this alive, I'm never speaking to my

parents again," Parker says. "I can't believe they sent me here. They were supposed to get references about this place!"

"Let's get out of here before something else catches fire," Samir says.

He heads for the stairs and the rest of us follow, even as the boat rocks violently from side to side. Up above us, the once blue sky is now dark and menacing, with lightning flashing in the dark clouds. The wind has picked up and whips through the sails, snapping them hard against their restraining ropes. Water sprays up from the choppy waves and I don't see land. Where it should be is blanketed with a thick fog.

Ryan helps Parker up the stairs. She still has a sprained ankle and is limping.

"I'm also going to sue," Parker says, mumbling a little. "I'm *still* going to sue. Definitely. I'll sue Bard, first, and then maybe my parents, second, but I'm going to sue. Oh, yes. For sure."

Parker sounds like she might be losing it.

"Where in hell are we?" Blade demands, bringing our attention back to the problem at hand.

We've somehow made it out to sea. Was Ms. P right? Is it possible to escape purgatory?

"Miranda!" I hear Blade shout behind me. I look back. She's pointing to the front of the ship. I look up and see Ms. P there with my sister. Ms. P is standing on the railing, a little like Leonardo DiCaprio in *Titanic.* She's holding her hands wide, as if trying to embrace the whale. My sister is standing next to her, holding the magical copy of *Moby-Dick* and reading from it.

That's how Ms. P is conjuring up characters as big as the whale and the ship full of sailors. By reading from the book, my sister can fully open the dimensions between reality and fiction. She's the key to everything. Just like I was when Emily Brontë hatched a similar plan last year.

I've got to get that copy of *Moby-Dick.* Without it, Ms. P will be powerless and we can send Ahab and his crew back to where they came from.

I try to make my way over to Ms. P and Lindsay, but the ship lurches hard to the right, slamming me into the railing. Just when I think I have my footing, I lose it again. It's like trying to walk in a funhouse, I just can't seem to make any forward progress.

"Lindsay!" I shout to try to get her attention, but she can't hear me over the gale-force winds.

Heathcliff, who's stronger than I am, grabs hold of the railing and holds his other arm out to me. I grab it, and together we move forward steadily.

Nearby, I see Ahab and a group of his crew members scramble into a small boat. For a minute, I think they're abandoning the ship, but then I realize they're all carrying harpoons. They're going to try to hunt Moby Dick in the storm. They're insane.

Ahab orders his men to lower the boat, which they do. I don't have time to bother with them. I fix my eyes on Lindsay and manage to make steady progress to her. Heathcliff is by my side, moving with me.

"Lindsay! You're going to get us all killed!" I shout at her. She turns, eyeing me warily. Ms. P whips around, too. "Give me the book."

"Don't listen to her, Lindsay," she tells my sister. "She's just jealous. Jealous of you and your power."

"You don't know what you're doing, Linds," I say. "You could end the world as we know it. You'll kill us, Mom and Dad, everybody."

I feel Heathcliff beside me, ready to spring. Blade and Samir walk cautiously forward. Ryan is busy holding up Parker, who is still clutching at him and mumbling.

"Don't come any closer!" Ms. P calls, holding out the copy of *To the Lighthouse* over the choppy ocean waves. It's Ms. W's book. If she destroys it, she'll destroy Ms. W.

We freeze.

Lindsay looks unsure suddenly. "Are they right?" she asks Ms. P. "Could we kill everybody? I mean, do you know for sure?"

"You're going to listen to them?" Ms. P sputters.

"After all the time they've ignored you? Taken advantage of you?"

"That doesn't answer my question," Lindsay says. For once, I'm glad she's got a know-it-all attitude.

Out of the corner of my eye, I see Ryan gently put Parker down on the deck. She sits there, cross-legged, leaning against the railing of the ship, silent. She looks a little dazed.

Ryan, meanwhile, tries to maneuver closer to Ms. P, sneaking over to her blind spot. Secretly, I cheer him on.

"I told you not to worry about it," Ms. P says, more sternly now.

"She told you not to worry about it because you'll be dead," Blade points out. "We all will be."

"It's true," I say, hoping to hold Ms. P's attention long enough for Ryan to get to her. "Tell her the truth, Ms. P."

But Ms. P isn't listening. She's caught sight of Ryan and she whirls around on him. With a flick of her wrist, she sends him soaring up off the deck and over the side of the ship. We all watch in amazement as he's flung into the churning sea.

"Ryan!" Lindsay shouts, louder than any of us. "No!"

Ms. P seems to realize her mistake. She was acting on protective instinct, but she's accidentally sent Lindsay's bargaining chip overboard. Lindsay now turns on Ms. P with a fury. "You bring him back!" Her face is red and I recognize a full-fledged temper tantrum coming. Ms. P senses this, too, and turns to look over the deck, searching for Ryan, but the waves are so choppy she can't see him. She can't levitate what she can't see.

I hope Ryan is okay, but the sea is stormy and I don't even see his head bobbing in the water. He's strong, though, and a good swimmer. He told me he used to lifeguard for a couple of summers back home.

Lindsay closes her copy of *Moby-Dick* and hangs it over the side of the ship.

"Save him, now, or I drop this book!" Lindsay stomps her foot to show she's serious.

Just then, Ryan's head pops up in a wave about twenty feet from the boat. Ms. P sees him, too, and reaches out her arm. He's suddenly floating above the water, dripping wet and coughing.

"There, you see? Now give me the book and I'll bring him over the side," Ms. P says.

"Don't trust her!" Blade calls out, but too late, because Lindsay hands over the book. Naturally, the minute Ms. P has the book in her hands, she drops Ryan back into the foaming sea.

"That's it!" says Parker, coming to for the first time, pulling herself up on her feet. She hobbles up to Ms. P and grabs the book out of her hands. Ms. P is so busy concentrating on Lindsay that she doesn't see Parker. "No one messes with *my* Ryan," Parker adds for good measure, as she gives our teacher a hard push. Ms. P totters and then falls over the side of the boat.

I feel a little like cheering for Parker. Except for the fact that she's Parker, and because one second later she drops *Moby-Dick* over the side of the boat.

"Parker! We needed that," I say. "There's no other way to curb the storm or get us home."

"I'll get it!" Lindsay shouts, scrambling up on top of the boat railing and leaning over, trying to reach the book. But, in seconds, Ms. P has appeared again, this time dripping wet and clutching both books to her chest—*Moby-Dick* and *To the Lighthouse.* With her free hand, she reaches up, grabs Lindsay's arm, and flings her overboard.

I'm not sure if it's Lindsay screaming, or me, as I run straight to the edge and look over. Miraculously, my sister's managed to fall straight into the boat with Captain Ahab and his crew, saved from the ocean, which—given the fact that she can't swim—is a good thing. She's out cold, though, and that's definitely bad. So is the fact that they're headed straight out to fight Moby Dick, and everything in the book says they'll lose.

"We've got to save her!" I shout to Heathcliff, who's already in motion. He leaps at Ms. P. She sidesteps Heathcliff's lunge, but isn't quite fast enough. He manages to grab a book from her hands and tosses it to Blade, who catches it easily. She pops open the book and Ms. W flies out.

"That's more like it," she says, then turns to face Ms. P, whose eyes widen in fear.

"Who's afraid of Virginia Woolf? I'd say *you,* right now," Blade says to Ms. P.

"Good one," Samir says.

"You think so?"

"Oh yeah, definitely." Samir nods his admiration.

"Would you two get a room already?" Parker snaps at them both. "Jesus. Enough with the flirting banter."

The two teachers circle each other warily and then, suddenly, Ms. P floats upward, toward the lookout post on the ship, fleeing as fast as she can go. Ms. W follows.

I am still hanging over the rail, watching Lindsay sail away with Ahab.

"Lindsay!" I shout. "Lindsay! Wake up!" Lindsay groans a little, but doesn't quite come to. I watch, helplessly, as Ahab's rowboat moves farther and farther from the ship. Beside me, Heathcliff glances at the water. There's too big a gap now to jump, even for him. I look out on the ocean and see that Ryan is swimming toward Lindsay. He's making good progress. I hope he gets there soon.

Above our heads, Ms. P and Ms. W clash.

"Give up, Sylvia, you're trapped!" Ms. W yells.

"Never!" Ms. P shouts back.

The two ghosts swirl in figure eights around the ship's mast and sails. At this rate, Ms. P could play her game of "keepaway" forever.

A bright light breaks through the clouds in the horizon. It's sunlight, and it slashes through the clouds in sharp rays, illuminating the water in bright, dazzling patches.

"We're at the boundary," Ms. W calls to Ms. P. "We can't go any farther."

"I assume she means purgatory?" Blade asks me.

"We can go farther and we will. I *will* see my children again."

Beneath our feet, the boat comes to a standstill. It's strange, but true. We just stop moving and the sea around us goes completely still. Behind us, the storm is still raging, but in this one spot, with the light coming down, everything is still. It's like we've crossed some invisible line. The ocean runs past us, but the boat is completely still, as if some large invisible hand is holding us stationary.

"Whoa," Samir says.

"This is *so* cool," Blade says, leaning far over the rail to watch the water splash up against the side of the boat, even though we're no longer moving.

I put my hand out over the rail of the ship and it hits something hard and cold. It's like invisible glass.

"I told you we were at the boundary," Ms. W says. "Now, stop this nonsense and come with me. You can go no farther."

"No," Ms. P says, floating out over the ship's stern. She puts her hands up as if to feel what is holding us in place. "No! It isn't possible! The ocean!"

"We cannot leave before our time," Ms. W says. She's nearly close enough to Ms. P now to grab her. She lunges, but Ms. P spins away at the last second and the two are suddenly locked in a struggle. Somehow Ms. P loses her grip on the book and *Moby-Dick* falls into the water beside us. I see it slowly sink beneath the surface. There's a giant bubbling circle, as if it's causing some kind of reaction with the water.

"Is that what I think it is?" Samir says, pointing.

The bubbles grow bigger, then a spout of water bursts up through the surface. A whale's signature.

I swallow, hard.

"If you're thinking it's the world's most famous sea mammal, then yeah, it's what you think it is."

We turn in time to see a massive white tail rise out of the water just feet from the boat. It stays there, still, for a second, dripping water, before crashing through the bough and sending splinters of wood in all directions.

Twenty-six

Chunks of wood and water fly through the air as the *Pequod* leans sharply to one side. The mast cracks in half and comes crashing down beside us as Parker, Heathcliff, and I hop one way to avoid it and Blade and Samir go another.

"No way, it isn't . . . it's not possible," Parker is sputtering in shock.

"Get used to the impossible," I say.

Moby Dick slides under the boat and it rocks hard to the left. I lose my footing and go sliding on my back across the deck, dangerously close to the water that's bubbling up from Moby Dick's attack.

Heathcliff shouts my name as he tries to come after me. But the deck is in pieces and it's hard for him to find his footing.

I don't see any sign of the whale, but I know he's nearby and that he can swallow people whole. I flail my arms and legs and manage to grab on to some fish netting. But it looks like I'm too heavy for the netting because it's coming loose from the hooks holding it to the ship.

At my feet, I see the water churning and bubbling. As I watch, frozen, the whale surfaces, its giant head huge and hulking. I'm now a few feet away from its massive, bent jaw. Its mouth creaks open, revealing rows and rows of razor-sharp teeth, each one big enough to cut me in half. I'm starting to think movie producers made a mistake when they chose sharks for *Jaws.* Moby Dick is way scarier.

"Um, nice whale?" I say, trying to get a firmer hold on the fishnet, which is coming loose in my grasp. And then I hear a scream and Parker tumbles down the deck, bouncing into me, and nearly sending us both into the giant mouth of Moby Dick.

She's now clinging to the net and I'm holding on to her legs.

"Don't let go!" I shout to her.

"Um, state the obvious!" Parker shouts back.

Moby Dick blows out more water from his blowhole and opens his mouth wider, sending out a scented bouquet of decaying fish.

"Geez, ever heard of an Altoid?" I say, flinching.

"What's an Altoid?" asks Ms. W, who swoops in from above my head and lifts us to safety.

"Ms. W! Thank God."

"You're welcome," she says as she puts us down on the edge of the ship that isn't yet underwater.

Parker just crosses her arms. "I'm still going to sue," she tells Ms. W. "And just because you're a ghost doesn't mean you're not liable."

I crowd together with Blade, Samir, and Heathcliff, who are all holding on to whatever they can to stop themselves from sliding into the bubbling water.

"Where's Ms. P?" I ask, glancing quickly around us.

"There," Ms. W nods. I follow her gaze backward to see that Ms. P is floating over the water. It looks like she's going after Ahab's boat, and Lindsay.

"We have to stop her. But where's the book?"

"That book?" Samir asks, pointing at the water, where a soaking-wet copy of *Moby-Dick* bounces up, buoyed by a wave.

"Exactly," Ms. W says, grabbing it from the water. She hands it to me. "I'm going to save your sister and get Ms. P."

"You have a plan?" Samir asks, hopeful.

"I'm going to lure Moby Dick over here and when I do, you have to capture him in this book, do you understand?"

"What's this about luring the whale *to* us?" Samir asks, looking unnerved.

"Um, I hate to point out the obvious here, but has

moby clique   255

anyone *else* noticed that this ship is sinking?" Blade asks, nodding toward the bubbling water, which seems to be eating up the deck.

"Hang on for as long as you can," Ms. W says. "I'll be back."

And with that she floats off in the direction of Ms. P and Ahab's boat. Ryan is in it, struggling with Ahab. He's trying to get control of the boat. I feel a swell of pride. Even if I'm over him, it's nice that he's on my side. And he sure is fighting hard to save my sister. And for once, I'm not jealous. I'm glad.

I can't see if Lindsay is awake or not and I can't see where the whale is, either. I watch as Ms. W grabs Ms. P from behind. There's a struggle, as Ms. W tries to contain Ms. P and starts pulling her back toward the *Pequod.*

"Oh no," I hear someone behind me cry. I look in time to see a large white hump coming toward us. It's Moby Dick.

"Um, is this the luring? 'Cause I'm not a fan of the luring," Samir says.

The ship, which is sinking fast, lurches even farther to one side as water bubbles up along the deck. Caught between the waves and the invisible barrier keeping us in one spot, the ship's deck begins to crack and break apart beneath our feet.

Suddenly, I'm losing my footing. Heathcliff tries to

steady me, even as he's pushing me farther back in the boat, away from the water. The boards beneath my feet buckle. I throw my hand up to grab something, anything, but all I get is air. I'm sliding backward. As if in slow motion, I watch the first edition of *Moby-Dick* fly right out of my hands and over the side of the ship's railing, making a little *plunk* sound in the water.

And then a strong hand grabs me—Heathcliff.

"The book!" exclaims Samir.

"I think I can still reach it," I say, grabbing a harpoon and leaning over the side of the quickly sinking ship. The hook at the end of the pole is just inches from the bobbing book. I can almost reach it.

"Too late," Samir says, holding on with both hands to the ship's mast. He nods forward and I see the white whale closing in.

Heathcliff scrambles across the deck and starts gathering together the harpoons that are left on deck.

"What are you doing?"

"Trying to save us," he says.

"At least someone is," Parker says.

The water along the deck starts moving quickly toward us as the ship lurches even more toward its broken half. I lean even farther over the edge of the boat. I almost have the book. It's *this* close. Millimeters, even.

Heathcliff grabs a rope and leaps up to the railing of the boat while the ship dips farther down. He steadies himself as the whale circles around what's left of the ship, then heads for us.

I've got a corner of the book under the harpoon's hook now. All I have to do is pull it in. I can almost reach it.

Moby Dick surfaces near the ship, blowing water high into the air. With a steady hand, Heathcliff takes the harpoon and aims straight at the whale's eye. He lets the harpoon fly and it hits home. The whale writhes and wiggles, as if trying to shake loose the sharp barb. Then, without slowing down, it flips over and dives deep.

Just as he does, I snag the book.

"Got it!" I shout, lifting it over my head.

And the next thing I know, Moby Dick hits us again with his massive tail. This time, the hull cracks in two. The ship is now breaking into small pieces and sinking fast.

"Jump!" Heathcliff says, grabbing my hand and pulling me overboard. Blade and Samir follow us into the water, where we all land with a cold splash. The frigid salt water stings my eyes, as I try to follow Heathcliff to nearby floating debris. Behind us, the small pieces of the *Pequod* drift apart, some sinking and some bobbing on the surface. Seconds later, barrels of water and a square box that looks a lot like a coffin pop up in the water. Parker manages to swim to it and grabs hold of it.

"I can't swim!" shouts Samir, sputtering and struggling in the water. Blade reaches him, though, and together they swim to a floating barrel of gunpowder.

Heathcliff points to them and I nod, swimming for another barrel nearby, all the while keenly aware that I'm in the middle of a freezing ocean with a wounded but angry Moby Dick swimming somewhere nearby. I'm clutching the book and trying to swim at the same time, but I'm not going very fast.

The water around me is so dark it's nearly black and I can't see anything below about a foot beneath the surface.

I try not to think about being swallowed whole. I am also seriously regretting ever seeing any of those lame *Jaws* movies, because right now all I can think about is the possibility of something chomping on my legs.

The sea swallows the top of the *Pequod*'s mast, the last bit of the ship disappearing under the black water. Debris floats everywhere, but there's no sign of the whale.

"Where'd he go?" Blade sputters beside me. Samir is clinging to her, his knuckles white.

"Do we really care as long as he's not *here*?" he points out.

"He's there," Heathcliff says, nodding toward Ahab's row boat, which is about thirty feet from us.

In fact, he surfaces right beneath Ms. W and Ms.

P. Somehow, Ms. W spins away just seconds before Ms. P is swallowed—whole—by Moby Dick.

"*That* had to hurt," Samir says.

"Gives a new meaning to the words 'fish food,'" Blade says. When I give her a look, she adds, "What? Samir is the only person allowed to make insensitive quips here? Besides, she's a ghost—can she even *be* eaten?"

"Looks like it," Samir says as Moby Dick dives deep underneath the water. He comes up again even closer to the rowboat—and my sister.

"Lindsay!" I shout, but I can't see her from where I am. Ryan is there, still squaring off with Ahab, who isn't giving up an inch. Most of Ahab's other men have fallen overboard or been pushed by Ryan, so now it's just him and the captain. Ahab swings a paddle at his head, but Ryan ducks. For a man with just one leg, Ahab sure can fight.

Ms. W picks up a bit of rope from the water and starts pulling the boat toward us. Moby Dick takes the bait and follows.

"Get the book ready," Heathcliff tells me.

I haul myself up on the floating debris with Samir and open the sopping wet book. The pages are all stuck together and the type has started to blur. I don't even know if it'll work like it's supposed to. But as soon as I start to doubt, the book begins to work its magic.

Pieces of the *Pequod* floating around us start getting sucked into the book like it's a giant vacuum.

"Miranda! Watch it!" Parker says as the coffin she's floating on zips into the book, nearly taking her with it. I shut the book, quickly.

"Sorry," I say.

"Wait until the whale is closer," Blade suggests.

"I would've appreciated that suggestion about five minutes ago," Parker says, bobbing to another piece of the *Pequod* and latching on to it.

Ms. W tugs the boat toward us. She's making good progress, but not good enough.

"She's not coming fast enough," Heathcliff says, nodding at Moby Dick, who has sunk down below the surface again. He's going to eat the rowboat, just like he did in the book. He's going after Ahab, and Ahab happens to be right next to my sister. Ms. W seems to sense this, too.

Ryan pushes Ahab, hard, and Ms. W grabs him, lifting him above the water and away from the boat—straight to us.

Moby Dick breaks off his attack on the rowboat and follows the floating Ahab, who is struggling against Ms. W's grip.

"Let me go, woman!" he's shouting. "The white whale is mine!"

"Miranda! The book! Open it! Open it now!" Ms. W yells.

"But what about you? You have to get out of the way!" I say, fearing that she'll get sucked into the book, just as surely as Ahab and Moby Dick will. I don't know the extent of the book's power.

"Don't think. Do it!" Ms. W yells.

I open the book and in a loud *whoosh,* nearby debris from the *Pequod* is quickly sucked into the book, as is a good amount of water from the ocean. The row-boat is pulled, but not drawn in, and I see Ryan cover Lindsay's body with his own to protect her from flying debris. I can barely hold open the book, the force is so great. Heathclliff steadies my hands.

The book pulls on the whale, who fights it, but quickly starts to lose ground. With one last great show of will, Moby Dick leaps forward and swallows Ahab and Ms. W whole before being sucked straight back into the pages of the book.

I shut the book abruptly, but it's too late. The whale and Ms. W have been sucked into the pages of the book.

I'm completely silent for a minute. I can't believe it.

"Whoa," Blade says.

"Yeah—whoa," Samir adds.

"Oh, I'm definitely going to sue the school," Parker says, rubbing her eyes, as if she can't believe what she saw. "I'll get seven figures, easy. High sevens. Maybe eights."

"Maybe I should open the book again, see if Ms. W pops out," I say, feeling a little sick and guilty all at once.

"Wait," Heathcliff says, putting his hand on mine. "We'll lose what little debris from the *Pequod* we have left."

"The H-man has a point," Samir says. "Unless you want to dog paddle back to Bard Academy."

"Um, are you guys going to just sit there or is someone going to tell me what the heck just happened?" This is from my sister, who is sitting up in the rowboat and rubbing her head. "And by the way, any of you dorks see my retainer around here?"

Twenty-seven

The rowboat, which amazingly was not sucked into the book, has Lindsay and Ryan in it. Ahab and his crew are gone. She scoots over to make room for us and Blade, Samir, Parker, Heathcliff, and I crawl in.

"Does anyone know which direction land is?" I ask.

Everyone looks baffled. I take that as a "no."

"Well, what *I* want to know," Lindsay says, "is just how long were you going to keep the Bard secret from me anyway? I mean, just *when* were you going to tell me *how frickin' cool* this school is?"

"Yeah, and you almost destroyed it and everything else," I say.

"Details, details," Lindsay says. "So is it true? Is our great-great-great-whatever a fictional character? And is Heathcliff *the* Heathcliff?"

"Yes and yes," I say.

"Okay, ghosts I get. Heathcliff I get. But *you* two,

no way," Parker says, shaking her head. She might be forced to believe that Moby Dick can come to life and that her teachers are ghosts, but accepting that the Tate sisters are special is simply too much of a stretch for her. I glance at Lindsay, expecting her to change her mind and agree with Parker, but she doesn't. Instead, she just pretends like she didn't hear her.

"So does this mean we have, like, superpowers or something? I mean, because if we do, I am *so* making an outfit and, like, getting an alter ego, 'cause, like, all superheroes have one and . . ."

"Is she every going to shut up?" Blade asks.

"Probably not," I say.

"Paddle! Everybody, let's paddle!" Blade commands.

Even with all of us paddling, we don't make it very far. And we're not even sure exactly the right way we should be headed, so we soon give up. There aren't exactly any landmarks way out to sea. Heathcliff suggests we conserve our strength and wait for rescue.

We float for another hour, at which point I don't know how much longer I can sit in this hard, uncomfortable little rowboat. Not to mention, it's sprung a slow leak, so the floor has an inch of water in it and my shoes are sopping wet and my toes are numb from the cold. And when my sister isn't talking about being a superhero, Parker is ranting about just how much money she's going to get out of the school when her father finds out about the purgatory thing. And no matter how often we try to tell her that you can't talk about Bard's secret outside campus, much less in a courtroom, she just doesn't believe us. Ryan is quiet and just stares out to sea. I don't know what he's thinking about, but I'm sure he's got the whole Rebecca thing to process. I don't have much time to think about it because I'm busy looking at Heathcliff, grateful he's still here. He sees me looking at him and covers his hand with mine.

"We'll be all right," he whispers in my ear and I believe him.

As more time passes, I start to think about Hana. I hope she got away from that guy in the woods. I can't wait to tell her about everything that happened. I sure hope she's okay.

"What do you think happened to Hana?" I ask Heathcliff. He shrugs. He doesn't know.

"I'm betting she got away," Samir says. "She's the fastest runner I know."

"She doesn't run fast," I protest. Hana is more of a bookworm than an athlete.

Samir shrugs. "Yeah, I know. I was just trying to make you feel better," Samir says. "But I still think she got away."

"We didn't see her on the *Pequod*," Blade points out. "So chances are she wasn't captured."

This is true and it makes me feel better.

"What about Ms. W?" Samir asks. "I mean, you think we can ever get her out of the book?"

"I don't know," I say.

"Who cares about your stupid little friends?" Parker sneers. "What about me? I think my ankle is broken. I know it is." She rubs it gingerly and I have to admit it looks bad. It's swollen and it's black and blue. Still, I'm pissed that she called Hana and Ms. W stupid. But I'm not surprised. Parker never thinks of anyone but herself. "Lindsay, would you give me your jacket, so I can elevate it?"

I half expect Lindsay to do it, even though it's freezing out, and the wind is blowing hard and we're all practically shaking from the cold. Lindsay, however, just pulls her jacket closer to her and wrinkles her nose.

"As if," Lindsay scoffs, clearly not letting go of her jacket anytime soon. Parker is shocked. Lindsay has never actually denied Parker anything before. I guess this means that Parker's hold on Lindsay is broken. Finally.

"I guess you'll have to find a new clone," I tell Parker.

"Oh, shut up, the both of you," Parker growls, put out.

Lindsay and I exchange a smile.

"Guys, how good does the Bard Academy cafeteria food seem right now?" Ryan asks, cutting through the tension to change the subject.

"Really good," I agree.

"You guys are pathetic," Blade says. "We're out here in the ocean and you're dreaming about Bard Academy food? How about some Taco Bell?"

"I would totally go for some Red Lobster," Samir says.

We all stare at him.

"You can't be serious," I say.

"What? All this talk about Moby Dick, it got me hungry for seafood."

"Wait, guys, what's that?" Ryan asks, pointing to the horizon.

We all look in the direction he's pointing and we see it. A huge ship.

"But I thought the *Pequod* was sucked back into *Moby-Dick*," Blade says.

"It was, that's something else," I say.

"It's the *Rachel*!" Samir shouts. "The *other* boat in *Moby-Dick*. The one that saves Ishmael."

"We're saved? We're saved!" Parker says. "Oh, thank God."

When the ship gets close enough, I see a familiar figure standing on deck. It's Coach H.

The *Rachel* slows down a bit and Coach H orders the crew to scramble into rowboats. In a few minutes, one of the boats paddles out to us.

And then I notice someone else who looks a bit familiar in the boat.

"That looks like . . ." Heathcliff starts.

"It can't be," I say, blinking hard.

"Hana?" Samir asks, unsure, as the boat gets closer to us.

"Ahoy, mateys!" shouts Hana. She's grinning from ear to ear, and is wearing what looks to be a captain's hat with a big white plume in it. "Did someone ask for a rescue?" she adds, stretching out her hand to me.

Twenty-eight

"Boy, am I glad to see you," I tell Hana as soon as I'm in the rowboat. "The sailors—I thought for sure they got you. But then, I didn't see you on the boat, so . . . *where* have you been?"

"Um, saving your butt, that's where I've been," Hana says, grinning. "As usual, you're the one getting into trouble and I'm the one saving you."

"*You* saving *me*? I don't know about that!"

"Anyway, those guys that were after us on the rock ledge weren't Ahab's men. They were led by Queequeg, who apparently staged a mutiny and went to work for the *Rachel.* He took some men with him, which was why Ahab was short on crew members."

"That didn't happen in the book," Samir says.

"Yes, well, change of plan in this version of the story," Hana says. "And Coach H was already on the ship when I got here. Those other Bard students who were kidnapped got back to campus and told him everything, apparently. So then we saved your sorry butts."

"Hey, watch who you're calling sorry," Blade says as we get to the *Rachel.* We climb up a rope ladder and onto the bigger ship. On deck, we come face-to-face with a tattoo-covered sailor who looks a lot more like a cannibal than a whaler. And he's beating a drum. So *that's* where the drumming sound came from? I guess that's one mystery solved.

Samir turns white, while Heathcliff stiffens beside me as if readying himself for a fight.

"Don't worry, guys, he's cool," says Hana. "*This* is Queequeg."

Blade and Queequeg study each other. He has more tattoos, but she has more piercings. The two seem to have a kind of mutual admiration for the other.

"Coach H, I just want you to know that as soon as we get back to shore, I'm calling the family attorney and we will sue the school for *everything,*" Parker snaps as soon as she's safely on board.

"You can try," Coach H says, giving me a knowing glance. "But I have to warn you that the students who've attempted to explain the secret away from Shipwreck Island ended up in mental institutions."

Parker sniffs as if she doesn't believe him, but then she slips into a stony silence.

"That's where she belongs anyway," Blade mutters.

"Well, a few counseling sessions with Ms. W ought to set her straight," Coach H says. "By the way, where is Ms. W? She went looking for you, and . . ."

I look down at my shoes and then I tell him the story of how she got trapped in the book. But Coach H, instead of seeming sad or upset, just throws back his head and laughs.

"Self-sacrifice! She's one sneaky gal, that Virginia," Coach H bellows.

"I don't get it," I say.

"She's gotten her ticket out of purgatory," Coach H says. "Self-sacrifice, you know. It's the one sure way to get out of here and straight to, well, someplace else. We're not sure exactly if it's heaven or nirvana or reincarnation. The next step, as it were."

"You're kidding. She's been freed?"

"What do you think?" Coach H asks us, holding up Ms. W's book *To the Lighthouse*. It's fading right before our eyes. Even as we watch, it disappears entirely. Coach H looks at his now-empty hand. "I'm gonna miss you, Virginia," he whispers to it.

"But what about Heathcliff . . ." Blade starts.

I elbow her in the ribs.

"What? Isn't it weird that . . ." She's about to tell Coach H that the last bit of *Wuthering Heights* was destroyed. I elbow her. I don't want to know how he's still here, I'm just glad he is. And I certainly don't want to freak the faculty out by letting them know he's bending the rules of the space/time/fiction continuum, or whatever you'd call it.

"Well, I hate to be the bearer of bad news," Coach H adds, clearing his throat, "but I'm afraid that after you and your friends went into the woods, that Ms. P called your parents."

"She *what!*" I exclaim.

"I'm afraid they're going to be waiting for us when we return."

It's a long quiet ride back to Shipwreck Island. There's a bus waiting near the shore to take us back to Bard Academy, where I get time to shower and change before meeting the 'rents. After getting dressed, I stop at Blade's door. I wanted to know what she was planning to tell her parents so we can all have our stories straight. Her door, which is unlocked, swings open after my knock and I catch a glimpse of Blade making out with a guy.

"Oh, geez, sorry!" I say, springing back.

That's when Blade and her new paramour sit up on her bed and I see, with a start, that she's been sucking face with Samir.

I must look completely shocked because Blade says,

"Hello? You didn't see this coming for three semesters?"

Samir, who's a little embarrassed at being caught, manages to rally enough to add, "Sorry, Miranda. I know you secretly had the hots for me, but I'm afraid I'm all about Goth this year."

I don't even register his joke. I'm too stunned.

"But . . . what about Hana?" I ask, thinking that she had a secret crush on Samir for ages.

"We're just friends," Samir says. "She's the one who told me to . . ." His face goes red. "Well, you know."

"Yeah, I did," Hana says, appearing next to me in the hall. "And I so *do not* have a crush on Samir, for the record. He's strictly friend material, I swear. But I didn't trust Blade to treat him the right way since she's pretty fickle about sticking with guys—no offense, Blade."

"Right, none taken," she says.

"But then I got to know her better and decided she was a perfect match for Samir. So I told him he ought to go for it."

"I am completely confused."

"Yeah, I know," Hana says, patting my arm sympathetically. "You thought you were the only one with a complicated love life."

Blade throws her arm around Samir, whose lips are covered with dark smudges from black Goth lipstick.

"I hate to be rude, but, uh, don't you guys have somewhere else to be?"

Outside the bell tolls, signaling free period. My parents! I'm late to meet them.

"Unfortunately, yes," I say. "Gotta go face the firing squad."

On the steps of my dorm, I nearly trip over Ryan, who's waiting there, backpack over one shoulder.

"I wanted to make sure you were okay," he says as he falls in step beside me.

"I'm fine," I say. "And by the way, thank you for looking after my sister. You really saved her out there."

Ryan blushes and looks away. "Oh, it was nothing."

We walk in an uncomfortable silence for a moment.

"Listen, I know you have a thing for Heathcliff," Ryan starts. "I mean, it's pretty obvious."

I look down, not meeting his eyes.

"But I think maybe, I dunno, maybe there is still something between us. What do you think?"

"I don't know what to say."

"Don't you feel it?" he asks me.

Ryan is gorgeous, no question. His blue eyes are staring a hole straight through me. But do I want to be his girlfriend? I just don't think so. It's Heathcliff I want. And Heathcliff I can't have.

"I just don't think it will work," I say, shaking my head.

Ryan nods, as if expecting this answer. I'm surprised he's taking this so well, but then again, I guess it was pretty obvious to him how I felt on the *Pequod*. I look up and see we're almost at Headmaster B's office. Lindsay is waiting for us, tapping her foot impatiently.

"I understand," he says. "But you know, if you change your mind . . ." he trails off. And before he can say more, Lindsay speaks.

"Miranda! You're late." Lindsay looks annoyed. She glances shyly at Ryan. "You can't expect me to face them alone!"

"Our parents are here," I tell Ryan, who looks disappointed that our conversation is ending.

"Well, good luck, okay?" he says to us both.

"Thanks, I'll need it," I tell him as he turns and walks back across campus. He gives me one last backward glance before continuing on his way.

As I swing open the door to the faculty hall, I nearly collide with Parker, who's hobbling out on crutches. Her eyes narrow in annoyance when she sees me.

"Parker! What are you doing here?" I ask, almost afraid to hear the answer.

"Just setting the record straight," she says, playing innocent.

I'm starting to get nervous now. There's no telling what Parker said in there.

"What did you say?" Lindsay demands.

"Well, let's just say that I told the truth. *My* version. Like how Miranda was the one who led us into the woods and that the entire thing was her idea and she's the one who recklessly endangered us all." She looks down at her hurt leg. "So she's the one responsible for my ankle. It was lucky we weren't killed because of her."

"But that's not true!" Lindsay exclaims.

I glance at her, surprised. It's not like her to stick up for me. I would've thought she'd be glad Parker paved the way for her to scapegoat me—again.

"Parker, I only went in the woods because I was worried about my sister," I say. "And you went because you wanted to keep an eye on Ryan."

Parker stares at me a long moment. "Well, it's your word against mine," she says finally. She hobbles past us and out the door. You'd think that the near-death experience we shared would've helped us bond, but as far as I can tell, Parker is as evil as ever.

Twenty-nine

"I can't believe I was ever friends with her," Lindsay says, shaking her head. Then she looks at me. "So you really were worried about me?"

"Of course, you dummy," I say. "You're my sister. Even if you are totally annoying almost all the time."

"And you came after me, even though you knew Parker was probably going to tell on you and you were going to get detention or worse."

"I wasn't going to let you wander around these haunted woods all by yourself. I had to do something to try to help you. I mean, that's what sisters do."

Lindsay falls silent a moment.

"Not that it matters," I say. "Mom and Dad are going to kill me anyway. I'm going to end up going to juvenile jail, just like Dad always says."

Lindsay sends me a sidelong look, then falls silent. We're in front of Headmaster B's door and I take a deep breath before I step inside. Headmaster B isn't anywhere to be seen, but that doesn't mean she's not lurking around somewhere. But my parents—both of them—are waiting. I haven't seen them in the same room since they were fighting over the divorce settlement.

Mom squeals and runs to Lindsay immediately, putting her in a big premenopausal Mom hug, and Dad follows suit with his own version of a hug. The two actually overlap arms in order to hug their favorite daughter. Neither one seems particularly concerned about me.

"God, are you all right? We were worried *sick* about you," Mom says, wiping away tears as she pulls herself away from the hug.

"They told us there were bears in the woods," Dad says. He even looks a little choked up. "And cougars! You could have been seriously hurt."

I can't believe this. I'm standing right here and I was in the woods, too. But neither one seems to care. Headmaster B drifts into the office then. I look at her, but can't tell what she's thinking. Her face is set in a carefully neutral expression. I wonder if Coach H managed to tell her everything that happened.

Dad turns his gaze to me.

"And you, young lady," he says in his most stern voice. "I thought we told you to *look after your sister*."

Yeah, I'm the one almost eaten by a giant whale and *I* get the lecture. Figures.

"Yeah, well, I thought you weren't supposed to be a walking cliché, but I guess we're both wrong," I say, referring to the fact that he ran off with not one, but two secretaries.

Dad's face goes red.

"That has nothing to do with this," he says, his eyes flicking to Headmaster B, wondering if she gets the reference. I turn to her to make sure she does.

"My dad likes to change wives as often as he changes his ties," I tell her. "And he always goes for his secretaries because, apparently, he's not even computer literate enough to use Match.com."

"That's *enough,* young lady," Mom pipes in. Figures she'd defend him. She always defends him, even though he's the one clearly in the wrong.

Both Mom and Dad are fuming now. This is why I am not the favorite.

Dad clears his throat and changes the subject.

"I've been talking with your mother about this and I think it's only fair that something be done about your reckless behavior," my dad continues. "We've looked into a number of ways to deal with this and we think maybe a juvenile detention center might be best."

"Dad . . ." Lindsay says, speaking for the first time.

Okay, here she goes. She's going to put the nail in

my coffin. This is where she talks about how it really is all my fault because I told her to go into the woods, or because I tricked her into it, or I pressured her, or was just basically a bad sister. And then, just for good measure, she'll tell both Mom and Dad that she thinks they're both great role models and that I have it all wrong.

"It's not Miranda's fault," Lindsay says.

I do a double take. Literally. Did she just say it's *not* my fault? Is this Opposite Day and no one told me?

Both Mom and Dad seem slow on the uptake. They look at Lindsay as if she has to be mistaken.

"But the other student—Parker—told us that this was all Miranda's plan. That she pressured you into doing this," Mom says.

"Mom!" I whine. I can't believe she took Parker at her word! "Why are you so gullible? You can't believe *anything* Parker says, she's a lying, conniving—"

"That's enough!" Dad thunders. "Miranda, don't talk back to your mother."

"I wasn't talking back. I was defending myself, there's a dif—"

"You say *one* more word and we're yanking you out of this school right now," Dad interrupts, his face red. God, I really hate him sometimes.

"Um, hello!" Lindsay shouts, trying to be heard. "As I was saying, it's not Miranda's fault. It's mine."

What? Lindsay admitting guilt? Did some alien kidnap my sister and replace her with some robot clone? Because the real Lindsay would never admit to wrongdoing under any circumstances.

"Surely you don't mean that," Dad says.

"Would you guys just listen for a second? Geez," Lindsay says, blowing hair out of her face in frustration. "Going into the woods was *my* idea, okay? Miranda didn't know anything about it. And when she found out what I did, she came after me to try to rescue me, even though it was dangerous and against Bard rules, because . . ." Lindsay pauses a little and sends me a knowing look. "Because that's what sisters do."

I'm stunned. And really touched at the same time. Despite being such a pain in the butt most of the time, I guess Lindsay really is a good sister. And she has done me a huge favor by fessing up for once.

"Well, this changes everything," Mom says.

"Hmpf," Dad grunts.

"And another thing, about driving through Carmen's store," Lindsay says. "Miranda never told me to do that. And it wasn't her bad influence, either. It was *my* mistake."

"I see," Mom says, looking back and forth between the two of us.

"Hmpf," Dad grunts again. He doesn't like it when

Lindsay admits guilt and he has to focus his anger somewhere else besides me. I'm such an easy target.

Lindsay and I stare at our parents for a long minute, waiting to see what they say next. They could decide to send us both to jail. Or they could take us both home. Or, who knows? I could be banished back to In the Puke.

Mom looks at Dad, who seems to be turning a lot of bright colors, none of which seem healthy. *"Hmpf,"* he says again.

"I think what your father is trying to say is that you've both learned your lessons," comes the calming voice of Headmaster B. "I think it's clear by Lindsay's more mature act of taking responsibility for her actions that Bard has been a good influence on her. And Miranda's strong sense of responsibility for her sister is evident in the fact that she risk life and limb to help her once she realized Lindsay was in trouble."

Both Mom and Dad still look a little shell-shocked, but they glance down at Headmaster B (who's barely four feet tall) and seem to register what she's saying.

"You're saying, then, that we should do *nothing*?" Dad barks. "That they've learned their lesson?" He's gritting his teeth, which means he clearly wants to punish us, and punish us badly.

"What I'm saying, Mr. Tate, is that these girls have a lot of growing to do and Bard Academy can help them accomplish that," Headmaster B says. "It's already working wonders for them, and a continuation of a strict regimen of study will help both of them become more focused. By staying at Bard, I think the two of them will benefit greatly."

"Hmpf," Dad grunts. He's still not able to form words.

"I think that's a splendid idea," Mom says, agreeing. Of course she does. She's easily persuaded by any figure of authority. For once, I'm glad about this.

"I thought you would like it," Headmaster B says. "I should also say that many of our faculty members think Miranda is making splendid progress. Some of them think she may have a great talent as a future writer."

"Yes!" Lindsay shouts, pumping her fist. "I get to stay!" Realizing her reaction was very inappropriate, she quickly becomes somber. She isn't supposed to be excited about the prospect of staying on another semester at a delinquent boarding school. "Er, I mean, yes, I'll have a lot of time to reflect on my mistakes at Bard," she adds, trying to look dejected.

"Ahem," Headmaster B says, clearing her throat. "Well, girls, I think you can head back to your dorm rooms. Your parents and I have a few more things to discuss."

Thirty

"Thanks for that," I tell Lindsay as we walk back to our dorms.

"Hey, whatever," she says, shrugging. "I only did it because I wanted to stay and I figured Mom and Dad wouldn't let me unless you were here, too."

"Figures," I say, giving Lindsay a playful nudge. "But you saved me from juvie jail anyway and I appreciate it."

"Don't mention it," Lindsay says. "And if you really want to repay me, you won't tell Mom and Dad about my broken retainer, either. They would totally flip."

"Secret's safe with me," I say, crossing my heart. "So you're going to stay away from Parker Rodham, right? She's bad news."

"Yeah, I know," Lindsay says. "I'm not totally clueless, you know."

"You know, you don't need friends like her to be popular," I say. "You're already pretty cool all on your own."

"I am?" Lindsay says, brightening for the first time and really smiling. I realize that she does care about what I think. Maybe more than I know.

"Of course you are," I say.

We smile at each other and I have to wonder if maybe Lindsay was so hostile to me all this time because she actually wanted my approval and just never got it.

"By the way, Ryan is still into you, you know," Lindsay says. She's trying to look like this doesn't bother her, but I know it does.

"I know. He told me."

"And so is Heathcliff," Lindsay points out.

"I know that, too."

"So which one are *you* into?"

"Well . . ."

"I'd *totally* go for Ryan," Lindsay continues, flipping her hair out of her face. Lindsay looks at me, to gauge my reaction.

"I'm just not that into him," I say. Lindsay looks visibly relieved.

"So it's okay if I date him, right?"

I look at her and roll my eyes.

"As if . . ." I say.

"As if, *what*? I am *totally* hot," Lindsay says, striking a ridiculous pose that looks a little like she ate something sour.

"Is that supposed to be your sexy face? 'Cause it needs some work."

"Shut up," she says, elbowing me. "You're one to talk. You're the one who's in love with a fictional character."

"So?"

"Speak of the devil!" Lindsay cries, looking off across the commons. "It's Heathcliff."

I look up and see him striding purposefully toward us. He's got his telltale scowl on his face.

"Why doesn't he ever smile?" Lindsay asks me.

"He does. Sometimes."

"I'll believe that when I see it," Lindsay says.

"Miranda!" Heathcliff says. "Do you have a minute?"

"Um, hello—are you going to even acknowledge my presence?" Lindsay pipes in. Heathcliff gives her a sidelong glance. "Um, right. Hello, Lindsay."

"Hello to you, too, Mr. Grumpy Pants."

I can't believe she just called Heathcliff "Mr. Grumpy Pants." How mortifying.

"Ignore her," I tell him.

"Whatever!" Lindsay sighs. "You guys totally need to loosen up. Anyway, I was just leaving."

She heads off toward the direction of her dorm, leaving me alone with Heathcliff.

He takes my hand and starts leading me off across the commons in the direction of the library.

"Wait, where are we going?" I ask him.

"Someplace private," he says.

"I wanted to talk to you, actually," I say. "Maybe we don't need to hide from the faculty anymore. I mean, your book was destroyed, and you're still here, aren't you? I don't know how. I mean, maybe it's just because you *wanted* to be, or because I helped you stay or something. Maybe I've got the power to keep you here forever?"

Heathcliff says nothing, he just looks at me.

"The faculty can't hurt you now, so we can, uh . . . well, I mean, if you want . . . we can, you know, go public, or something . . ."

This isn't going like I pictured it. For some reason, I can't say "date." It's like I'm physically incapable of saying that word. I'm starting to sound like a babbling idiot. Heathcliff saves me.

"There's something you need to see," Heathcliff says.

I let him lead me to the library. Once there, he promptly heads down the book aisle where the vault is located.

The vault is the special storeroom where all the

magic books are kept—like the copy of *Moby-Dick* that Ms. P used—first editions of classics that can bring fictional characters to life. I found the vault last year and, ever since, the faculty has forbidden me to go near it.

We're standing at the entrance to the vault, a rarely used row in the back of the library. The vault entrance is invisible to the naked eye. Heathcliff reaches up on a shelf and grabs a copy of *Crime and Punishment*. After tipping the book, a door in the floor slides open, revealing a stone staircase leading down.

"But I'm not supposed to—" I start.

"Shhhh," he tells me, looking about for any sign of the librarian. Seeing none, he pulls me down with him.

"If you're just doing this to make out with me, I swear . . ."

Heathcliff says nothing as the vault door slides shut above my head. We descend downstairs and I notice the vault looks much the same as it did last year. Eerie blue flames flicker in torches strung up along the walls. There's shelf after shelf of dusty old books. They don't look like they could bring fictional characters to life, but they can, even though some of them seem to be falling apart. The room smells musty and old.

I can't help but feel a little wigged-out down here. There's a scratching noise in the corner. We both jump and Heathcliff pushes me into a nearby row of shelves, putting his body in front of mine, as if to protect me.

"What is it?" I whisper, holding my breath. I ask this even though I know it could be anything. Last time I was in the vault I ran into Dracula. You never know who might be lurking around the corner down here.

Heathcliff waits a second or two and then, near our feet, a rat runs by.

"Ewwww," I sigh. "I think I'd rather see Dracula."

Heathcliff gives me a stern look. "Okay, maybe that's an exaggeration," I admit.

We're still chest to chest and I can feel Heathcliff's body pressed into mine. The next joke I was about to make dies on my tongue. Heathcliff is staring at me with those dark eyes of his that are so hard to read. His scowl is replaced by something softer as he traces my face with his forefinger.

"Miranda . . ." he starts.

My heart speeds up. "Yes?" I half close my eyes, expecting him to kiss me. But when I'm hanging there for a long second and nothing happens, I open my eyes again. He's looking at me sadly.

"That last piece of *Wuthering Heights* isn't the last piece," he says.

"What do you mean? I saw Ms. P light it on fire. And the rest of the book burned last year. We all saw it. When Emily Brontë disappeared."

That's when Heathcliff slides a book off the shelf in front of me. The title on the spine is *Wuthering Heights.*

"But that's not right. That can't be right. I saw this book burn." I turn it over in my hands. It feels real enough.

"Well, somehow it's back here," Heathcliff says. "Don't ask me how."

"So the faculty could banish you. If they wanted to."

Heathcliff nods.

My shoulders slump. Guess there's no way we can go public with our relationship.

Heathcliff puts one finger underneath my chin and pulls it up. I'm staring into his deep, dark eyes. They're even softer now, kind even. I can feel mine well up with tears. I thought he was here to stay, but this book means that he could go at any time. Without warning. Without even a good-bye.

"We knew this wouldn't be permanent," Heathcliff says, wiping a tear from my cheek. "But that doesn't change anything. You know how I feel about you, Miranda."

I nod.

"And I know how you feel about me," he says.

My eyes dart up to meet his. He does? Then again, I guess I've been a little obvious on that score.

"There's nothing I can do about this," he says, taking the book out of my hands and placing it back on the shelf. Then he takes both my hands in his and puts them on his chest. It's hard and broad and warm. He stares at me intently.

"But we can make the most of the time we do have. However long that may be."

"You're right," I say, blinking back tears and swallowing the lump in my throat. "I know you're right."

"It's not all bad," Heathcliff says, pulling me closer, the hint of a smile tugging at the corner of his mouth. "Now, how about you kiss me?"